P9-CFQ-206

THE GIFTS
OF THE BODY

used

THE GIFTS
OF THE BODY

REBECCA BROWN

HarperPerennial
A Division of HarperCollins Publishers

A hardcover edition of this book was published in 1994 by HarperCollins Publishers.

THE GIFTS OF THE BODY. Copyright © 1994 by Rebecca Brown. All rights reserved. Printed in the United States of America. No part of this book may be used or reproduced in any manner whatsoever without written permission except in the case of brief quotations embodied in critical articles and reviews. For information address HarperCollins Publishers, Inc., 10 East 53rd Street, New York, NY 10022.

HarperCollins books may be purchased for educational, business, or sales promotional use. For information please write: Special Markets Department, HarperCollins Publishers, Inc., 10 East 53rd Street, New York, NY 10022.

First HarperPerennial edition published 1995.

Designed by Nancy Singer

The Library of Congress has catalogued the hardcover edition as follows:

Brown, Rebecca, 1956–
    The gifts of the body / Rebecca Brown. — 1st ed.
        p. cm.
    ISBN 0-06-017159-6
    1. AIDS (Disease)—Patients—United States—Fiction. 2. Visiting housekeepers—United States—Fiction. 3. Home health aides—United States—Fiction. I. Title.
PS3552.R6973G53 1994
813'.52—dc20   94-5060

ISBN 0-06-092653-8 (pbk.)
95 96 97 98 99 ❖/RRD 10 9 8 7 6 5 4 3 2

CONTENTS

THE GIFT OF
SWEAT

I went to Rick's every Tuesday and Thursday morning. I usually called before I went to see if he wanted me to pick up anything for him on the way. He never used to ask me for anything until once when I hadn't had breakfast and I stopped at this place a couple blocks from him, the Hostess with the Mostest, to get a cinnamon roll and I got two, one for him. I didn't really think he'd eat it because he was so organic. He had this incredible garden on the side of the apartment with tomatoes and zucchinis and carrots and he used to do all his own baking. I also got two large coffees with milk. I could have eaten it all if he didn't want his. But when I got to his place and asked him if he'd had breakfast and showed him what I'd brought, he squealed. He said those cinnamon rolls were his absolute favorite things in the world and he used to go to the Hostess on Sunday mornings. He said he'd try to be there when they were fresh out of the oven and get the best ones, the ones from the center of the pan, which are the stickiest and softest. It was something he used to do for himself on Sunday, which was not his favorite day.

So after that when I called him before I went over and asked if he wanted anything, he'd still say no thanks, and then I would say, "How about the usual," meaning the rolls and coffee, and he'd say he'd love it.

So one morning when I called and asked him if he wanted "the usual" and he said he didn't, I was surprised.

He said, "Not today!" He sounded really chirpy. "Just get your sweet self over here. I got a surprise for you."

I said OK and that I'd see him in a few. I made a quick cup of coffee and downed the end of last night's pizza and went over. I was at his place in half an hour.

I always knocked on the door. When he was there he'd always shout, "Hello! Just a minute!" and come let me in. It took him a while to get to the door but he liked being able to answer it himself, he liked still living in his own place. If he wasn't at home I let myself in and read the note he would have left me— that he had an appointment or something, or if there was some special thing he wanted me to do. Then I would clean or do chores. I used to like being there alone sometimes. I could do surprises for him, like leave him notes under his pillow or rearrange his wind-up toys so they were kissing or other silly things. Rick loved surprises.

But this one morning when I knocked on the door it took him a long time to answer. Then I heard him trying to shout, but he sounded small. "Can you let yourself in?"

I unlocked the door and went in. He was in the living room on the futon. It was usually up like a couch to sit on, but it was flat like a bed and he was lying on it.

I went over and sat on the floor by the futon. He was lying on his side, facing away from me, curled up. His knees were near his chest.

"Rick?" I said. I put my hand on his back.

He didn't move, but said, "Hi," very quietly.

"What's going on?" I said.

He made a noise like a little animal.

"You want me to call your doc?"

He swallowed a couple of times. Then he said, "I called UCS. Margaret is coming over to take me to the hospital."

"Good," I said, "she'll be here soon."

"Yeah," he said. Then he made that animal noise again. He was holding his stomach. "I meant to call you back," he said, "to tell you you didn't need to come over today."

"That's OK, Rick. I'm glad I'm here. I'm glad I'm with you right now."

"I didn't feel bad when you called." He sounded apologetic. "It was so sudden."

"Your stomach?"

He tried to nod. "Uh-huh. But everywhere some."

He was holding the corner of his quilt, squeezing it.

"I was about to get in the shower. I wanted to be all clean before you came over. It was so sudden."

"Oh, Rick," I said, "I'm sorry you hurt so much."

"Thank you."

"Is there anything I can do before Margaret gets here?"

"No." He swallowed again. I could smell his breath. "No thank you."

Then his mouth got tight and he squeezed the quilt corner, then he was pulsing it, then more like stabs. He started to shake. "I'm cold," he said.

I pulled the quilt over most of him. It had a pattern of moon and stars. "I'm gonna go get another blanket," I said.

"Don't go," he said really fast. "Please don't go."

"OK," I said, "I'll stay here."

"I'm so cold," he said again.

I touched his back. It was sweaty and hot.

I got onto the futon. I slid on very carefully so I wouldn't jolt him. I lay on my side behind him. I could feel him shaking. I put my left arm around his middle. I slipped my right hand under his head and touched his forehead. It was wet and hot. I held my hand on his forehead a couple of seconds to cool it. Then I petted his forehead and up through his hair. His hair was wet too. I combed my fingers through his wet hair to his ponytail. I said, "Poor Rick. Poor Ricky."

He was still shaking. I pulled my body close to him so his butt was in my lap and my breasts and stomach were against his back. I pressed against him to warm him. He pulled my hand onto his stomach. I opened my hand so my palm was flat across him, my fingers spread. He held his hand on top of mine, squeezing it like the quilt. I could feel the sweat of his hand on the back of mine, and of his stomach, through his shirt, against my palm. I could feel his pulse all through him; it was fast.

I tightened my arms around him as if I could press the sickness out.

After a while he started to shake less. He was still sweating and I could feel more wet on the side of his face from crying.

When Margaret came we wrapped his coat around him and helped him, one on either side of him, to the car. Rick hunched and kept making noises. I helped him get in and closed the door behind him while Margaret got in the driver's side. While she was fumbling for her keys I ran around to her and asked her, "You want me to come with you?"

She said, "You don't need to. We'll be OK."

Rick didn't say anything.

I leaned in and said, "Your place will be all clean when you come back home, Rick."

He tried to smile.

"I'll call you later," said Margaret. She put her hand up and touched the side of my face. "You're wet," she told me.

I touched my face. It was wet. "I'll talk to you later," I said to her.

"I'll see you later, Rick," I said.

He nodded but didn't say anything. His face was splotched. Margaret found her keys and started the car.

I went back into his apartment. When I closed the door behind me I could smell it. It was a slight smell, sour, but also partly sweet. It was the smell of Rick's sweat.

I started cleaning. I usually started in the kitchen, but as soon as I set foot in there and saw the kitchen table I couldn't. I turned around and stood in the hall a second and held my breath. After a while I let it out.

I did everything else first. I stripped the bed and put a load of laundry in. I vacuumed and dusted. I dusted all his fairy gear, his stones and incense burners and little statues and altars. I straightened clothes in his closet he hadn't worn in ages. I untangled ties and necklaces. I put cassettes back in their cases and reshelved them. I took out the trash. I did it all fast because I wanted to get everything done, but I also wished I could stretch it out and still be doing it and be here when he came home as if he would come home soon.

I cleaned the bathroom. I shook cleanser in the shower and sink and cleaned them. I sprayed Windex on the mirror. When I was wiping it off I saw myself. My face was splotched. My t-shirt had a dark spot. I put my hands to it and sniffed them. They smelled like me, but also him. It was Rick's sweat. I put my hands up to my face and I could smell him in my hands. I put my face in my hands and closed my eyes. I stood there like that a while then I went to the kitchen.

What was on the kitchen table was this: his two favorite coffee mugs, his and what used to be Barry's. There was a Melitta over one full of ground coffee, all ready to go. There were two dessert plates with a pair of cinnamon rolls from the Hostess, the soft sticky ones from the center of the pan.

I thought of Rick going down there, how long it took him to get down the street, how early he had to go to get the best ones. I thought of him planning a nice surprise, of him trying to do what he couldn't.

Rick told me once how one of the things he missed most was Sunday breakfast in bed. Every Saturday night he and Barry would watch a movie on the VCR in the living room. They'd pull the futon out like a bed and watch it from there and pretend they were at a bed-and-breakfast on vacation. Rick would make something fabulous and they'd eat it together. That was when he was still trying to help Barry eat. After Barry died Rick started going to the Hostess, especially on Sundays, because he had to get out of the apartment. He used to go to the Hostess all the time until it got to be too much for him. That's about the time I started coming over.

I sat at the table he'd laid for us. I put my elbows on the table and folded my hands. I closed my eyes and lowered my head and put my forehead in my hands. I tried to think how Rick would think, I tried to imagine Barry.

After a while I opened my eyes. He'd laid the table hopefully. I took the food he meant for me, I ate.

THE GIFT OF
WHOLENESS

M rs. Lindstrom lived in a house in a different part of town than most of the people I worked with. I took the bus there. It was a neighborhood of nice small houses with yards. There were dogs and bikes and trikes and American cars in people's driveways. Mrs. Lindstrom's mailbox was painted red to look like a barn. The windows of her house had tied-back frilly curtains.

When I knocked on the door she answered immediately. She'd been waiting for me. I was glad I was exactly on time. She opened the door and said, "Hello! Come in!" and put out her hand for me to shake. She ushered me in and said did I want coffee or tea. She didn't say it like it was a yes-or-no question but an either-or.

I said, "Coffee, please," and she motioned for me to follow her into the kitchen. Her clothes were loose. She had curly white hair. She walked with a cane but steadily.

She told me to have a seat at the kitchen table so I did but she didn't. She leaned against the counter, her hands on either side to steady her. She put one hand over her chest like she was saying the pledge. She was breathing hard.

I got up. "So, is the coffee in the canister?"

There was a set of matching canisters on the counter.

"I'll get it," she said breathlessly.

I hadn't meant to rush her but I didn't want her waiting on us. I sat back down. There were two matching cups and saucers out on the counter.

She gripped the edge of the counter and took deep breaths.

I looked around the kitchen. "You have a lovely house," I said.

"Thank you," she wheezed.

She asked me if I'd had breakfast, which was what I usually asked them. I told her I had, and before I could say anything else, she said she had too but maybe I was hungry after the bus ride. "You did take the bus, didn't you?" she said.

She was still trying to catch her breath, so I said yes, then told her a very long, detailed story about how I could have taken the 10 or the 43, or even the 7, to downtown, and how I got the 43, and where I got it, and where I got off downtown to change, and where I caught the 6, and about asking the bus driver for her street etc., etc. I stretched the story out until she was breathing evenly. I finished by saying what a nice neighborhood she lived in.

"Thank you," she said. "I've lived here my whole life."

She turned around to get the coffee and tea. The coffee was a jar of instant. I wished I'd asked for tea.

Margaret had told me Mrs. Lindstrom's kids had tried to get her to move in with them, and that her son had said he'd move back home with her, but she wouldn't have either. She would let her kids do medical things like take her to appointments and medicine errands, and she let the nurse come see her at home, but she wouldn't let her kids take care of her body, like feeding and bathing, or of her house, like cleaning. But when it got to where she really couldn't cope at home alone if she didn't get some help, she finally gave in. I was her first home care aide.

She got the tea out. I heard her lift the lid from the canister and pull out a tea bag. She unscrewed the lid of the coffee jar and clicked the spoon in and put it into the cup. It took her a long time to do everything.

She started talking. She asked me where I lived in town, in a house or an apartment, if I had pets and so on, all nice polite questions someone that age would ask. She pulled a plate of cookies from the cupboard and took the plastic wrap off and put them on the table. When she sat down she was breathing hard again.

She said the cookies were homemade, her own recipe, but by her daughter Ingrid. She said to help myself to a cookie. I took one and said, "Thank you."

She didn't take one. Then we didn't say anything. I heard myself chewing.

When the water boiled she got up for it. Her hand looked tight on the kettle, her veins were sticking up. She was working hard to lift it. I wanted to offer to help but I knew not to yet. She wanted to feed me.

She poured water into our cups and took the kettle back to the stove.

When she sat down again we stirred our coffee and tea for a few seconds. Then I said, "Well, Mrs. Lindstrom, what can I help you with today?"

She looked down at her lap, "Oh. Yes. Well. Let's see." She looked out the kitchen window. "What would you like to do?"

No one had ever asked me what I'd "like" to do before.

"Well . . . ," I said, "do you have some laundry?"

"Oh, don't trouble with that," she said.

"It's no trouble," I said. "I like to do laundry."

She put her hands around the edge of her saucer and said, "Well, maybe I can find some laundry for you."

I asked her where the machine was. She made me finish my coffee and eat another cookie and told me she kept the hamper in the bathroom and the soap and bleach and machines were in the basement. She said she'd go down and show me, but I told her I could find them myself and if I had any questions I'd ask her.

Then I said, "Maybe I can clean the kitchen while the laundry's in."

"Oh, that's all right, you don't have to." She looked around and said, embarrassed, "Do you think it needs it?"

I didn't want to make her feel bad by saying that her kitchen did need work, but it did. There weren't dirty dishes in the sink, or open cans of food around, but the counters and floors looked coated.

"I'll just tidy up a bit while the laundry's in," I said.

"Well . . . all right," she said, "if you're sure it's no trouble."

"It's no trouble at all, Mrs. Lindstrom," I said.

She mumbled something about not cooking much lately, not being in the kitchen much. Then she said stiffly, "Well, I guess I'll get out of your way," and got up to go. She set her hands on the edge of the table and took a deep breath and pushed herself up. I stood and started to take her arm, but she waved me away.

She went into the living room and I took the laundry down to the basement. On my way back to the kitchen I looked in the living room. She had the *Today* show on and was sitting in one of the two big overstuffed armchairs. She had her knitting stuff in her lap, but her eyes were closed.

When she heard me going by she looked over at me. "Are you finding everything you need?" she asked.

"Yes, ma'am," I said.

"There's not much in the fridge, but please help yourself to anything. There's all those cookies."

"Thanks," I said.

The kitchen was full of cooking things, but nothing was being used. In the fridge were a couple of dried-out casseroles in dishes that didn't match hers, a bunch of wrinkled fruit and vegetables, lots of yogurts way past their sell-by date, and a case of Ensure hi-cal protein drink.

I went there in the mornings three days a week and stayed till noon. Sometimes I was there when the nurse arrived, but I tried to be gone before he did. Mrs. Lindstrom didn't feel comfortable around the nurse and me together. The nurse was there for medical reasons, there was no getting around that. But sometimes it could seem like I was just there to help around the house, like a companion or a maid or even a neighbor who drops by when you have the flu. But it couldn't seem like that when the nurse was there too.

There's something about no one else knowing someone is taking care of you. When UCS, Urban Community Services, started and people were afraid their neighbors would panic if they knew they had AIDS, you weren't supposed to tell anyone exactly what you were doing. You'd say, "I'm a friend." But when I saw the nurse or he saw me, Mrs. Lindstrom couldn't have the illusion that no one knew she was being taken care of because she was sick.

The first weeks I was there I cleaned most of her house, except her bedroom, which she felt very private about, and ran errands and went grocery shopping and cooked things she said she used to like and sat down with her when she ate and that's when we talked. She asked me where I'd gone to college and what my interests were and about my family and hobbies and pets. She told me about her family, her three kids, Diane and Ingrid and Joe. Joe, her youngest, was just two years older than me. There were four grandkids and a fifth on the way. She had pictures of all of them plus of Miss Kitty, who'd moved in with Joe and Tony when Mrs. Lindstrom got sick. Mrs. Lindstrom said she truly missed Miss Kitty, and laughed that she'd only really gotten serious about knitting when Miss Kitty adopted her so Miss Kitty would have something to play with. Miss Kitty came along after John, Mrs. Lindstrom's husband, passed away. She said that when John died she was devastated, like she'd lost her whole life. They'd been sweethearts at the local high school and had lived with each other their whole lives. But then after he died she made herself do things, like the Animal Shelter and the Literacy Program and the Neighborhood Block Association.

She started spending tons of time with Ingrid's twins. "I missed him so much," she told me. "I didn't know how I would survive when he died, but I did."

After she told me all that she told me to call her Connie instead of Mrs. Lindstrom. That took me a while to get used to, but I did.

Then after I'd called her Connie for a while, she said would I help her with her bath. That was the last thing she'd kept doing herself. I said, "Sure."

I ran the water in the tub and put in some bath oil. I kept the door closed so the bathroom was warm. I went to get her when everything was ready. We walked down the hall together. I carried her clean clothes. She held her cane in one hand and kept her other hand on my arm.

We got in the bathroom and closed the door. She sat on the toilet seat. I helped her undress. She hadn't let me dress or undress her before.

When she opened her blouse I couldn't help the look on my face.

"You don't have to help me with this," she said.

There was a big flat dent on half her chest, and a long white scar where they'd cut it off. The scar wasn't shiny, but it was old. They'd cut it off before they tested the blood supplies.

"You don't have to help," she said again. "I bathed myself alone when I had my mastectomy."

They'd cut it off before there was Urban

Community Services. She didn't get help recovering. But even if she had had her surgery when there was UCS, she wouldn't have gotten our help because it couldn't be a mastectomy or only cancer or something else, it had to be AIDS. I felt ashamed.

"I can do this alone," she said again.

I hadn't moved since I saw it, but when she said that, I said, "I can help," and she let me.

I helped her off with the rest of her clothes. Her other breast was shriveled and small. I tried not to look when I covered her with a towel.

She didn't look right without her clothes. Her body wasn't whole.

I put my hand in the tub. I touched the water to the inside of my elbow to test the temperature the way you do when you wash a baby.

I helped her to stand and walk to the edge of the tub. We dropped the towel. I lifted her arm and put it around my neck. She held on to me tight, and we sat her on the edge of the tub.

"Are you all right?" I asked.

"Yes," she said.

I held her there a few seconds, then lifted her body and slid her onto the bath seat. She gripped the handles on both sides of the seat. The veins in her hands stood out. She was holding her breath and her shoulders were tight. I lifted her legs and put them in the water.

After a while she let out her breath and her shoulders relaxed and she said, "Oh, this water feels nice."

I soaped the sponge and washed her arms. I washed her neck and back and stomach. When I got to her ribs I hesitated. I was afraid about the scar.

"It doesn't hurt anymore," she said.

Then I could wash the place around the scar.

When she was clean I helped her out of the tub and patted her dry and got her into her nightie. We walked her to her room. She pulled my arm around her waist and leaned on me to walk.

She sat on the bed and gripped the edge. She was breathing hard. I lifted her feet and helped her lie down. I held the back of her neck and laid her against the pillow and pulled the covers up. I tucked the covers around her close, the way my mother did when I was young.

THE GIFT OF
TEARS

I was at Ed's the day they called to tell him they had a room. He'd been on the waiting list for a while, and we had called them every day to see when he could move in. Ed was always saying, "Well, I won't need to worry about that after I move . . ." Or "I better take care of that before I move . . ." Everything was divided into Before and After the move. But when he got the call and they had a room for him, he didn't want to go.

He was on the couch watching *The Young and the Restless* and I was dusting the shelves. The phone was nearer to me, so when it rang I picked it up and handed it to him. He took it, and I punched the TV remote to turn the volume down enough so it wouldn't interfere with the call but still be loud enough to hear so that when he got off the phone and said, "OK, what'd I miss," I could tell him.

But this time when he got off the phone he didn't say anything. He just hung up and sat there.

"Who was it?" I asked.

"The hospice." He took a deep breath. "They have a room."

"Yeah," I said cautiously. "You've been waiting for a while."

He looked at the TV. "Can you turn it up?"

"Sure." I clicked up the volume.

"What'd I miss?"

"Not much," I said. "She's still about to tell him the baby isn't his, but she still hasn't." There was this actress on the screen with long black curly hair and a diamond necklace and she was blubbering away to this actor. She kept sniffing and wiping her eyes.

"I bet she won't tell him till next week," Ed said. He pulled the blankets up.

"What about the room?" I said.

He kept looking at the TV. His eyes didn't change when the commercials came on. They were showing two white socks, but one was really white. "I told them I'd call them back," Ed said. He looked at the socks. There was a kid playing football. "They told me to call back this afternoon," he said. When the commercial changed to dog food his voice changed. "They won't even let me think about it overnight."

"I think they need to give the room to someone else if you don't want it," I said. The hospice was partly funded by how many beds were occupied every night. Also, there was always a waiting list.

"Oh," he said. He was still looking at the TV. Then he said all at once how his sister was coming next week and she was taking time off from work and arranging for her kids to stay with a friend so she could see him and he didn't want to be in some hospice. He said he still needed to have his garage sale and that Lee was having a party and he hadn't made an appointment with the carpet people and he still hadn't found the right buyer for his car. "So I can't go yet," he said, "I've got too much to do."

I came over and sat next to him on the couch. I handed him the TV remote. He took it in both his hands.

"Your sister can stay here while she's in town," I said, "even if you're at the hospice. And we can take care of the garage sale and find a buyer for the car."

"What about the party?" he said. He sounded about four years old.

"You can go to parties from there," I said.

"What if I want to leave? I mean, just go out by myself for a while?"

"You're allowed to do that," I said. Ed hadn't been out alone in months.

He switched the channel to a nature show. He never watched nature shows.

"I'm getting better," he said. "I got better at the hospital, I just needed a boost. I put on three pounds."

"Yeah," I said, "that was really good."

He'd just gotten back from the hospital two days before. In the previous six weeks he'd spent more time in the hospital than out of it. He always felt better when he came home from there. They pumped him full of IV and wouldn't let him leave until he felt better. He also felt better when he came home because he liked being around his things. But he'd also lost a pound since he'd come home.

"I *am* feeling better," he said. "I'll put on more weight when my sister comes. She'll cook for me all the time, I'll put on tons." He was begging, like this four-year-old for a pony.

He wasn't getting any better. He was just getting worse more slowly.

"I don't need to go to the hospice yet," he whined.

I nodded. "Well," I tried to sound casual, "you could take the room but keep your apartment too." Which was only partly true. The rules were that you could only keep your apartment until the end of the month that you moved into the hospice. But I really thought he should go.

He was watching a bunch of people running around with spears on TV. "If you get any better do they let you come back home?" he asked.

"Sure," I lied.

No one ever came home from there. No one ever got better.

"Sure," I lied again.

He stopped looking at the TV to look at me. He laughed. "Like hell."

I wanted to say something, I didn't know what,

but he turned up the TV. Everyone was screaming and running with their spears.

After a bit I said, "Do you want to talk to your case manager?" I had to say it loud over the TV. He stared at the TV. "Or Margaret?"

When the scene switched to the spears flying he said, "Do what you want."

I went into the bedroom and called his case manager. I told him the hospice had called with a room but Ed didn't want to go, and he said to give Ed time. He said sometimes people didn't want to go when it actually came down to it. I said Ed was supposed to call the hospice back this afternoon. I asked him what he thought. The case manager said he thought Ed should take the room but it was his own decision.

I went back to the main room. Ed had turned to another soap.

"This poor thing is just bawling her little eyes out," Ed said. "I bet she's gonna have someone's baby too that she doesn't want to tell." He looked at me with this fake sad look in his eyes and said, gooey sweet, "Pooooor thing."

I sat next to him and watched the TV. The end titles of the show were coming on, and the awful music.

"Tune in tomorrow!" Ed said, really chirpy.

"Ed," I said.

He started humming along with the music, bobbing his head and shoulders back and forth like an idiot.

"Ed," I said again.

"OK, OK," he snapped. "What?"

I started to tell him some of what the case manager had said but he interrupted me.

"I'll call them in a while," he said. "I'll call them in my own good time."

I watched the end of the titles with him. When the show was finally over and there was a station break I asked him if he wanted anything.

"Make me something to eat," he ordered. He'd never sounded like he was giving orders before.

"What would you like?" I said.

"Every fucking thing in the fucking house," he said. "Pancakes, syrup, fruit, bacon, orange juice, milk, eggs—two over easy—half a cantaloupe, oatmeal." He actually had all that in the house. Then he said, prissy-sounding, "Eggs benedict, rack of lamb, a fruits de mer soufflé, huevos rancheros, quail eggs, chanterelle mushrooms au jus, and a petit filet mignon, s'il vous plaît."

He looked at me. I didn't say anything.

"All right," he shouted. Then quietly, apologizing, "Oatmeal?"

I went to the kitchen and fixed him the oatmeal. I tried to calm down while I was stirring everything in.

Ed didn't look up from the TV when I brought

him his tray. I put it down in front of him and arranged his silverware and napkin and the sugar and milk.

"Where's my tea?" he said.

"I'll get you some," I said.

"I always have tea," he said. "You should know that by now." He didn't always have tea. And when he did he usually had it separate, after he ate.

"I'll bring it now, Ed," I said.

"My oatmeal will be cold by the time I get my tea," he said.

"I'm sorry, Ed," I said. I went back to the kitchen.

"I can't eat unless I have my tea," he shouted at me.

"OK," I shouted back. I took a deep breath. I wished I was better at this. "It'll only take a second!" I tried to sound nice.

I made the tea. I made a cup of coffee for myself. I brought the tea and coffee out. I put his tea down in front of him. I was going to drink my coffee and sit with him while he ate, the way we always did.

"Go clean the bedroom," he said. He didn't look at me. His hands were in his lap, clasped together.

"All right," I said evenly.

I took my coffee into the kitchen and got the vacuum from the hall closet and went into the bedroom.

When I came out to put the vacuum away he said from the couch, "I called them." He said it in a regular speaking tone, so I almost didn't hear him. I came into the room and sat down next to him.

He muted the TV. "I'm not going," he said.

I made myself not say anything, but I couldn't hide how I looked.

"I told them I might come later," he said. He stared right at me. "You can't force me to go."

"No one's trying to force you, Ed. We just thought—"

"I don't care what you 'just thought,'" he said. "I don't care what any of you—Margaret or my stupid case manager or my doctors or any of those fifty-five thousand asshole nurses or idiot orderlies or any of you fucking do-gooders think. I'm not going."

In training they said if they ever got "verbally or physically abusive" you should leave. But this wasn't that. Ed's face looked tight. His hands were gripping the remote control so tight he was shaking. The knuckles were white.

"I'm sorry, Ed," I said.

It took him a few seconds. Then he said, "You don't know what it's like."

"I know I don't, Ed. I'm sorry."

His mouth moved. He picked his spoon up off the napkin. The oatmeal hadn't been touched. He held the spoon in his fist like a baby who can't hold it in his fingers yet. His mouth was shut tight. His eyelids were red. He put the spoon toward the oatmeal. A skin had formed on the surface. He stuck the spoon through the skin. He made a noise like he was starting to cry.

"Oh, Ed," I said.

He put his hands against the bowl like he wanted to push it away. I moved to push it away.

"No, leave it," he sobbed. "I can eat it, I want to eat it."

"Do you want me to heat it up," I said, "or make you a new bowl?"

His lips were pressing very tight, the edges of them looked white. "I don't know," he sniffed, "I don't know, I don't know."

He dropped his spoon and put his face in his hands. His shoulders shook.

I touched his shoulder. He dropped his hands from his face and looked at me. His face and eyes were red. His mouth was moving. The rest of him was trying to cry but something was wrong with his tear ducts and he couldn't.

THE GIFT OF SKIN

Margaret said she was sorry to call me on a Saturday but the guy's regular person couldn't make it so she needed a sub and could I help out. The guy only lived a few blocks away from me. His name was Carlos.

A guy named Marty let me in. He was a friend who'd been staying at Carlos's place at night. Marty had to go to work during the day. Margaret had told me all that on the phone. Marty said hi and ushered me into the kitchen, gestured at the fridge, the cabinets, the stove. Marty was a pudgy pear of a guy, mid-thirties, but he still looked like he had his baby fat, and that baby skin, like he almost never had to shave. His skin was pale white, his arms especially. He was wearing a short-sleeved shirt. He showed me his work number by the phone and another number for a guy named Andy. He showed me the hall closet with towels and laundry soap, cleaning stuff, pads, sheets, gloves.

"There's more gloves in the kitchen above the sink," he said, "and in the bathroom."

"Thanks," I said, "I brought my own too." You go through a lot of gloves.

Marty showed me the room he stayed in. It was small and very plain. It wasn't really his room, he explained, just where he stayed. It was really Carlos's guest room, but he never had guests anymore. There was nothing on the walls. And just a single bed like in a kid's room, a chair, and a little table for a desk. No dresser. The closet door was open, and there were only a couple of shirts and a pair of pants. Marty said I could sit in the room and read or whatever because there was not actually much to do.

"Carlos likes to sleep a lot," Marty said. "Anyway, here's the newspaper. I only did half the crossword."

"Thanks," I said, though I always took a book to read.

We went down the hall. Marty said really loudly, "Here's the bathroom." We went in and he closed the door and whispered, "Carlos has been incontinent lately, so we just got this condom catheter. The nurse put it on last night. She said I should change it this morning. I didn't do it yet. I've never done one." He looked away from me. "You've done them before, haven't you?"

"Oh, yeah," I said. "No problem."

It was usually simple. Usually you just had to empty the bag. And even when you had to change the condom part, you just had to be careful, but it wasn't complicated or dangerous or anything.

"How about his meds?" Marty asked.

"Sorry," I said. "Can't do it. I'm not authorized." It was something about insurance. "But I can remind him, open his jars or med tray or whatever. He's got a tray, right?"

They usually did by the time they were in this shape. It was a plastic box with little sections for morning, midday, evening, night, where you put all the pills they needed to take at those times.

"Yeah," said Marty, "it's by his bed. I've given him his morning stuff. He'll just need his noon stuff."

"Right," I said.

"So," Marty said, "come meet Carlos."

We went back through the hall and kitchen and out to where Carlos's bed was set up in what used to be the living room. The room had a nice black leather couch and chair set, a big TV and VCR, a CD player, and billions of CDs. There was a huge yellowing plant as big as a little tree, and a bunch of other plants that didn't look much better. There was a wall of venetian blinds that were closed. The couch had been pushed toward the center of the room. The bed was behind the back of the couch. It was a hospital bed. The head was cranked up part way. Carlos was covered with a sheet up to his neck. His face was thin. He had a patchy beard.

"Carlos," said Marty. "Carlos?"

He opened his eyes. They were brown and watery. Marty introduced me to Carlos.

"Hi, Carlos," I said. I stepped close to the bed, careful not to knock the urine bag hanging from the side. The IV pole was on the other side. He wasn't on anything just then. I stuck my hand out to shake. It took him a second to get it, then he slowly pulled his right arm out from under the sheet. It was very thin. He didn't have on a shirt. His skin looked washed out, like it used to be darker but now it was pasty. His arms and chest were hairy—black, straight hair. I took his hand and did something between a shake and a squeeze.

"Hi." His voice was small.

"I'm glad to meet you, Carlos." I put my left hand on the back of his so both of my hands were around him. He didn't pull back. You can feel it when they want to, even if they're too weak to move. I kept holding his hand. It was clammy.

Marty told Carlos I was going to be there till two, when the nurse would come. "I've shown her around," Marty said to him, "so just let her know if you want anything, OK?"

"OK," said Carlos. He was used to saying OK to everything. He couldn't really object.

"OK. Bye, Carlos." Marty turned to go. He was halfway to the door when Carlos said, "Bye!" suddenly and very loudly. His eyes were opened wide like he was startled.

Marty came back. "I'll see you this evening,

THE GIFT OF SKIN

Carlos," he said slowly. He was trying to reassure him. He wanted to believe it too.

I felt Carlos's hand move. Marty looked at me.

"I'm gonna walk Marty to the door, Carlos," I said. "I'll be right back." I let go of Carlos's hand and laid it on top of the sheet.

At the door Marty gestured for me to step out into the hall. He closed the door behind me.

"My work number is by the phone," he told me again. "Call if you need anything."

"I will," I said.

"If Carlos wants to talk to me, you may have to dial for him," he said.

"OK," I said.

"And if you call and I'm away from my desk, leave a message, or they'll page me, or you can call our friend Andy. Andy's number is there too."

"OK," I said again. He didn't want to leave.

Marty looked at the door behind me. "Yeah . . . well . . . so. . . . You saw the urine bag and everything?"

"Yeah," I said, "I can change it right now."

He looked down at the carpet. "Carlos is embarrassed about the condom catheter. He won't be difficult, but—" Marty paused.

"I understand," I said.

Marty sighed. "The whole idea of him needing the damn—excuse me—the thing."

"That's OK," I said.

"It's another step."

I nodded.

"Everything's another step."

I nodded again.

"Like everything new is something else you've lost." He shook his head then looked down at his watch. "Oh gosh, I really gotta go." He started down the hall but turned back. "If you want to call to just check in with me, that's fine too. It's fine to call me at work."

"OK, Marty," I said again, "I will."

He stood there like he was trying to remember something. He really didn't want to leave but he forced himself to. "Right. OK. Well, now I'm gonna go. Bye," he said very quickly, and he went.

When I went back in, Carlos's eyes were closed. His mouth was slightly open and his breath was jerky. His hand was still above the sheet.

I went to the bathroom and washed my hands and put on some gloves. I found a white plastic pan and took it to the living room. I put it under the urine bag and closed off the tube and opened the bottom valve and the urine drained into the pan. The urine was orange. I closed the valve and made sure the bag was still hooked securely and took the pan to the bathroom and emptied it into the toilet. I cleaned and bleached it and put the pan back. I took off my gloves and tossed them in the trash and washed my hands.

I don't know how I could hear his voice over the water, but I did.

"Marty!" he was trying to shout, "Marty!"

I ran to the living room.

"Marty?" he said. His eyes were fluttering.

I took his hand. "Marty's at work. He'll be back later."

He squinted at me. "Who are you?"

I told him my name. He looked completely blank.

"I'm from Urban Community Services. I'm gonna be with you for a while until the nurse comes. Marty won't be back till after work."

He kept looking. After several seconds he said, "Oh." Then, "We met earlier?"

"A few minutes ago," I said.

He thought about that for a while. "Where were you now?"

"In the bathroom. I was washing my hands." I held my hands out, palms up, and flipped them over like a kid for inspection. "I didn't have time to wash behind my ears," I said.

That took him a few seconds, then he got it and laughed and said, "Very good."

His laugh was rusty. It was great to hear it. I laughed too.

He took my left hand in his right. "Your skin feels

so clean," he said. He pulled his other arm out from the sheet and took my other hand. "Your skin feels so clean."

I got a big blue dishpan from the kitchen and cleaned it and filled it with warm water and bath oil. I got a pile of fluffy clean towels and washcloths and a clean set of sheets. I put on a new pair of gloves. I rearranged things on the bedside tray. I put the med tray on the couch.

"You can sit up if I help you, right?" I said.

"I think so," he said.

"OK. I'm gonna ask you to put your arms around my neck and hold on, and I'm gonna put mine around your back and lift you a little and move you."

"OK."

I lifted his hands and put them on my neck. He was stiff and his skin was sticky. I put my arms around his back. I could feel his ribs against my forearms and his spine against my wrists. He was very thin.

"Are you all right?" I asked.

"Yeah," he said, but his voice shook.

"OK," I said, "now I'm gonna pull you toward me a little so you can sit up. Then I'll hold you up while I rearrange your pillows and move the bed some."

"OK." He sounded like a child being brave.

The bed hummed when I pushed the button to make it go up. He held my neck tight. My skin pulled. I stopped the bed when he was sitting up.

"How are you doing?" I asked.

"Fine." He breathed out heavily.

I waited a second. "OK. Now let's turn you some so your legs can hang down the side of the bed."

He nodded.

I tightened my hands around his middle, lifted him slightly and turned him. I heard him take another deep breath.

"You OK?"

"Yes," he said loudly, determined.

"You're doing great," I said. "Now just one more little move and you'll be set. I'm gonna pull you a little toward the edge of the bed so I can put your feet in the pan."

"OK."

But then the sheet lifted off him. "Oh God," he said. He dropped his arms from my neck and covered his dick and the condom part of the catheter with his hands.

"Excuse me," he mumbled.

I looked away to let him cover himself.

"You all right?" I asked after a few seconds.

He didn't say anything. Then, "Yeah, I'm OK now."

When I turned back he'd covered his lap again with the sheet.

I put a towel across his shoulders. "Tell me if you

get cold," I said. The place was stuffy. I was sweating in my t-shirt. I moved the pan and tray with everything closer to him. "Ready?"

"Uh-huh," he said.

I took his palms on top of mine and held them loosely, the way my father did when I was afraid of water and he was teaching me to swim. I held my palms beneath his and lowered them into the water. His hands slipped in with me. I could feel his hands tremble. I held his hands until they were still. I could feel the shape of him, the texture of his skin made smooth by water.

I looked at him. His eyes were closed.

"This is so nice," he said.

I slipped my hands out from beneath his. His stayed in the water. I swished the water around. The light made shifting lines on his skin. I dunked a washcloth and touched the backs of his hands with it.

"I'm gonna wash your arms, OK?"

"Uh-huh."

His eyes stayed closed.

I squeezed the cloth under the water then pulled it up his forearm to his elbow.

He took a deep breath. "Oh, that feels so nice."

I cupped water in my hands and poured it down his arm. I washed his elbows and arms and toweled them dry. I washed the hollows of his armpits and his ribs. I washed his back and stomach and shoulders.

When the water began to cool I filled the pan again with fresh warm water and fresh clean oil. I did his neck and face. I washed his forehead and eyelids and around his beard and mouth. The air began to smell like oil, like mint or eucalyptus.

I sat on the floor and washed his feet. I poured the water over them.

He looked down at me. He touched my head. His face was full of kindness. "Thank you," he said.

When we finished I didn't have to tell him how we needed to move because his body gave to mine. When I lifted his arms he put them around my neck. Our skin felt clean. I put my arms around his back and laid him down. I lifted his legs onto the bed and straightened the catheter tube. I took off the old top sheet and covered him with a towel. I turned him on his side away from me. His body was heavier than it looked, but he moved easily. I undid the near side of the old bottom sheet and put the new sheet halfway on. I rolled him toward me. His skin through my clothes felt cool and clean. I rolled away the old bottom sheet and spread the other half of the new sheet down. I laid him on his back. He was breathing hard.

"You OK?"

"Yes," he panted. "Just a little tired."

I flipped the clean top sheet out and tucked it into the end of the bed and up part of the sides. I slipped his towel off, careful of the catheter tube, and pulled the sheet up.

I was pulling the sheet up to cover him when he stopped me with his hand.

"Don't cover me yet," he said. "The air feels good, I want to feel the air against my skin."

THE GIFT OF HUNGER

Everyone tried to fatten her up. People brought her casseroles and baked goods and takeout. I could see who'd been there by what was in the fridge. A casserole with pasta and tomatoes and ricotta meant Joe and Tony. A giant paper plate of ribs or a box of Kentucky Fried or a big waxy cup with a plastic lid and two-thirds of a chocolate shake meant some of the kids from the Literacy Program. Homemade chocolate chip cookies meant Ingrid and the twins.

I used to try to be gone when the nurse came at noon, but after we'd overlapped enough times so that Connie couldn't pretend she wasn't getting home care and nurse visits all the time, I stayed till the nurse got there. It became important to stay so I could talk with the nurse a little before I left.

It was morning rush hour when I got off the bus near her house. I saw her neighbors going to work and they got to know me and ask, "So how's Mrs. Lindstrom?" and I'd say, "She's had a good couple days." Or, "Oh, you know . . ."

I checked her mail on the way in. Her little barn mailbox had a weather vane for when there was something for the postal person to pick up. This day there was a package neatly wrapped in a brown paper bag and postmarked Vermont. Plus one of her newsletters and the usual junk mail. She looked at all of it. She said the junk mail kept her up on what was really going on out in the world. Sometimes we looked at the catalogs together because she wanted my opinion on things for her kids.

I knocked on her door and shouted, "Hello!" and let myself in with my set of her keys. The TV was on to the *Today* show. She thought Bryant Gumbel was such a nice young man, and the only one who could ever hold a candle to Barbara Walters.

Connie was lying on the couch. Sometimes, because the couch was beige and the blankets were beige too, and because she was so small, you almost couldn't see her lying there until you saw her face.

"Morning, Connie," I said. I dropped my pack and jacket on the table.

She shouted good morning over the TV and pulled her hand out from the blanket to wave. The light coming in the window behind her caught on her diamond wedding ring. Sometimes I worried it would slide off, but she didn't want to put it anywhere for safekeeping because she didn't want to take it off.

I took the mail over to the couch and asked her how she was doing.

"Fine," she said. She always said she was fine.

"Well, you're gonna feel great when you see your mail." I helped her sit up a little and handed her the package. She looked through the bottom of her bi-focals. Her eyes widened.

"Oh!" She sounded really happy. "It's from Diane!"

Diane was her daughter in Vermont. She was married to Bob. They had two kids, Robert and Maria, and were expecting a third.

"Can you get me the scissor?"

The sewing box was on the footstool next to the couch. She didn't do the sewing or knitting she used to, but she kept her things close for when Tony came over for his bootie-knitting lessons. He was thrilled about Diane and Bob's new kid. Connie also kept the knitting close in case she felt like it. I got the scissors out of the box. They were in an old leather safety cover. I handed them to her handle first.

She snipped the string and tape on the box. I watched the joints of her fingers work. She was still pretty deft. She folded the flaps back and reached down through the foam peanuts.

"Oh, isn't this darling," she said.

It was a can of Vermont maple syrup shaped like a house with a triangular roof. The lid sticking up was supposed to be the chimney. The can was painted with a house, a guy in overalls and a red cap, trees and buckets. There was also an envelope: "For Grandmommy." She slipped a scissor blade under the flap and opened it. She put the scissors down on the couch and started to take the card out but stopped and picked up the scissors and said, "Can you put these away?"

I put them back in their leather case, then back in the box. Connie kept all these habits from having children in her house.

When the scissors were safe she pulled out the card. It had a pencil drawing of maple leaves colored outside the lines with red and orange and yellow crayons. She opened the card. There was a photo inside.

"Oh, don't they look precious!" she said.

I looked over her shoulder. I recognized them all from the photos she'd shown me before. She had pictures everywhere of all the kids at different ages and a few of her and John. She used to be fat.

"So Diane's letting her hair grow," she said. Then she held the picture at arm's length and squinted above and below her bifocal line. "Do you think she's showing yet?"

I looked. "Nah, not yet." It was only a few weeks since Diane had called to tell her mom she was expecting. I didn't know exactly when she was due.

"Well, Bob certainly looks nice with a beard, don't you think?" I nodded but she was still looking at the picture. "Look how Maria is shooting up! Maybe

Maria really will be Bob's basketball star . . . and sweet little Robert."

In the picture Maria's arm was around her little brother. They were all in red caps and boots and plaid jackets like the guy on the can of syrup.

"Oh, how absolutely darling," she said again. Then she started to read the card. I gathered up the wrapping paper and foam peanuts. I was about to wad them up and toss them when she said, "You want to save that box and packing material?"

"Oh, sure," I said. Connie saved everything.

"Wrapping things go in the hall closet on the shelf behind the vacuum."

"OK," I said. I folded the paper and put it and the peanuts back in the box and went to the closet.

When I came back to the living room she told me the family news from the letter. I felt like I knew these people.

She picked up the can and held it close then arm's length away and started to read the label: "One hundred percent pure Vermont maple syrup. Great on pancakes—" She stopped.

I sat next to her and finished reading. "—French toast, and waffles. Try it on ice cream."

"Oh, Miss Kitty would love that," she laughed. Miss Kitty, her old cat, had a terrible sweet tooth.

Then she got this look on her face. She picked up the photo again. "You know why they sent me this?"

I didn't tell her what I was thinking.

"Well, I'll tell you," she said. She leaned back on the couch. I fluffed a pillow behind her. She closed her eyes and took a deep breath. I grabbed the TV remote and muted the volume. She was holding the can and the picture tight in her hands. Her skin had brown age spots. Her veins were thick and blue.

"Joe took this trip in junior high," she started. "With the Glee Club. He loved the Glee Club. You know, he still has a beautiful voice."

She told me how the Glee Club went to a ski lodge and gave a concert. It was the first time most of the kids had ever been on a trip like that and they were crazy with excitement. The morning they were to come home they had a huge pancake breakfast. Joe always had an appetite, she said. Then, when Joe got home, he kept going on and on about the trip and the breakfast and how great the pancakes were. All the Lindstroms got tired of Joe going on so much and they said their mom, meaning Connie, could make pancakes just as good, so she made pancakes and Joe said they were good but not *as* good. Everyone else thought the pancakes were great so John—she used to refer to him as her late husband, but now she just called him her husband, or John—so John pulled out a different bottle of syrup from the cupboard and tried that, but Joe said they *still* weren't as good. So the next time Connie went to the store she got another

THE GIFT OF HUNGER

kind of syrup and Joe still said they weren't as good. It was already a joke. No one ever expected Joe to say his mom's pancakes were as good as they were on the trip. But after that everyone in the family would give Joe then everyone in the family including Joe, would give everyone else in the family, for Christmas or birthdays or their anniversary or even when there wasn't an occasion but just for a present, syrup. Connie said they knew, even the kids when they were young, that it wasn't the pancakes or even the syrup that mattered, but that their family had this special present they gave one another.

"So that's why Diane sent me the syrup," Connie said.

"That's great," I said. "It's a wonderful story."

I gave her a second, then I said, "So. You wanna try some syrup?"

"Of course! I'd love to!" she said with forced enthusiasm. "But I'm not hungry right now."

"OK," I said. "I'll get you your juice and maybe you'll feel like something in a bit."

"All right," she said.

I brought her juice in a big glass without a straw. She liked it when she could drink without a straw. Her new med tray was on her couchside table. She put the syrup and card and picture on the table and I handed her the med tray. She put it on her lap and opened the morning section. She took the meds out one by one.

She needed to take them with lots of fluids and she also needed to take them slowly, so this took time. She liked me to sit and talk with her while she took her meds. So I sat next to her and told her about what I'd done the last couple of nights and what I was going to do that weekend. She used to say she liked hearing what young people were up to these days and she passed on to her kids what I told her. I never talked with her about other people I worked with.

Occasionally she said things between her meds but not often because she had to concentrate. She had to be very slow. Sometimes if she was taking an especially long time I tried to encourage her a little, but not too much, because I didn't want her to feel worse like she was also a failure because she was so slow.

After the last med, she drank down all the rest of the juice in the glass. That was good.

"Well," I said, "you ready for some of that syrup and pancakes?"

She hmmmed and clicked the TV back up. "Not just yet. . . . I'll let this settle for a while."

"That's a good idea," I said, as if she'd just come up with that excuse for the first time. "How about if I go tidy up the bathroom?"

I called it "tidying up" rather than "cleaning" so it didn't sound so big or necessary. I went to the bathroom and got out the cleaning stuff. I started with the tub.

Joe usually called her every morning during his break. They talked about what was on the *Today* show and how he was doing and if there was anything he could bring her when he came over. I ran into Joe a few times out and about. He was a sweet guy and so was his boyfriend, Tony. Once Joe told me he felt guilty, like he was the one who should be sick, not his mom. Both he and Tony tested negative. Joe said he knew he shouldn't feel guilty but he did. He said his mother had never done anything wrong and didn't deserve it. I told him he'd never done anything wrong either and that nobody deserved it. It sounded preachy as soon as I said it and I wished I hadn't but Joe just looked at me. He knew his mom didn't blame him. She didn't blame gay guys. She didn't even blame the blood banks, and she could have. But Joe didn't hold what I said against me. He always told me thanks for helping his mom and how glad they all were that she had someone she liked so much and that she finally let someone help her. She never let her kids help her with some things.

When I finished tidying up the bathroom and came out she told me that Joe called and she told him about Diane sending the syrup.

"Hey, you ready for some of that?" I said as if I hadn't asked before.

She hesitated. "Not quite," she said. "But how

about a cup of tea? And fix yourself some coffee and we can sit and visit."

"Great idea," I said. I went to the kitchen and put the water on. I spooned some of my French roast I'd brought to keep at her place into a filter and got out a packet of mint tea. I straightened up the kitchen while the water boiled. There was a new casserole in the fridge—looked like a Tony job, macaroni and ham and cream. There was one spoonful out of it.

I watched Connie through the window between the kitchen and the living room. The TV was on but she was looking at the can of syrup.

After the water boiled I took her cup of tea in. I left my coffee in the kitchen. I put the tea down on her table. She leaned over it, blew on it, lifted it to her mouth, and took a little slurp. She held the tea in her mouth a few seconds before she swallowed it.

She sat a while, then exhaled and said, "Oh, that tastes good."

"Good," I said. I stood there.

"OK," she said firmly. "Let's try some pancakes and syrup."

"You got it," I said.

"It was so nice of Diane to send it," she said. "I'm really going to enjoy it." She nodded like it was a done deal. Then she said, "And fix some for yourself."

I put my hand out for the can of syrup to heat up.

She hung on to it a few seconds more then gave it to me.

"Thanks," I said, "but I ate before I came."

We had tried lots of different ways. For a while I used to eat with her because it's easier for them sometimes if someone else is eating too. As if you're dining, not just eating to stay alive. But I'd stopped eating with her.

She reached over for her knitting stuff. She dropped the basket. A ball of yarn and a square fell on the floor. I picked them up and handed them to her.

"Thank you," she said.

I went to the kitchen to start the pancakes. I watched her in the living room. She was straightening the knitting stuff in the basket. A couple of times when I first came I'd asked her not to get her knitting all set up while I was fixing something for her to eat because it would only take a minute. But then I realized she did it to calm herself.

I poured pancake mix in a bowl. I added milk and egg and Ensure. There was a case of it in the fridge. You were supposed to try and put it in everything. I cooked the pancakes in lots of butter and threw in a huge handful of blueberries. I poured the syrup into a little pitcher and heated it up in a pan of water. I drank my coffee while I flipped the pancakes. When they were almost done she said, "You know, I think I could eat an egg too. Can you do me an egg on the side?"

"Coming up, ma'am!" I shouted in my short-order-cook voice. She got a kick out of this. Then I sort of sang, "Ooh-vereasy!" which was how she liked them. It was great that she wanted an egg.

I looked at her. She was clicking away at the knitting. That was truly great.

I put two pancakes and the egg on a plate and the syrup and butter and silverware and my coffee on a tray. I took it all to her couchside table and put it down in front of her. She packed up her knitting and tucked it beside her. I moved her tea to the corner of her table to make room for the food. The cup was still full.

"Anything else?" I asked.

"No thanks." She looked at the food a few seconds. "This looks great," she said. "Maybe even Joe would approve of these!"

"Maybe," I laughed with her. But I stood there.

She took a deep breath. "All right, Connie," she said to herself, "dig in."

She started to cut the pancakes. The tendons in her hands were white.

I had stopped eating with her after a while because it didn't help. She'd talk while I ate. The most she would do was stir her food around. So then we changed to where I'd fix her breakfast but I wouldn't sit with her while she ate because she didn't want me to see so I'd go clean some other room.

But she ate hardly anything when I wasn't there so we talked again and finally she said she was embarrassed. She said she didn't want anyone to see her like that—this was before it got so bad all the time—and we came up with this agreement that I could sit with her while she ate but only if I promised to not try to help or ask her if I could help afterward unless she specifically asked me to help. She never asked.

She didn't want anybody around because she didn't want anyone to see. Also, it was one of the few things she still did alone, that she thought she still could do alone.

She poured warm syrup over part of the pancakes. She was careful not to waste the syrup. She put the pitcher down and picked up her fork and got a little bit of pancake. She chewed it a long time before she swallowed. I swigged a gulp of coffee and looked at the TV.

A few seconds after she swallowed she said, "These are terrific! These are really delicious!"

"All right!" I said. I hoped I didn't sound too relieved. "You think they'd pass the Joe test?" I joked.

"They might," she nodded. "They just might." She looked down at the plate. She took a deep breath, let it out, took another bite, chewed, swallowed. For the third bite she tried some egg. I was still looking toward the TV, but I could hear what she was doing.

On the fourth bite I heard her hold it in her

mouth. After a few seconds she swallowed some but not all of it. Then after a few more seconds she swallowed the rest of it. I took another gulp of coffee. She asked quietly, as politely and normally as she could, "Could you please take this away?"

"Sure," I said. I tried to sound normal too. I loaded the plate and everything on the tray.

"They're really delicious," she said. "You're a terrific cook." She didn't want to hurt my feelings.

"Hey, Connie," I said, "it's OK. Really."

As I was taking the tray back to the kitchen she said, "I wonder if maybe in a little bit I could try some oatmeal."

"Great!" I said. I wondered if that would be better. Sometimes oatmeal worked when nothing else did.

In the kitchen I put the dishes by the right sink and started the water boiling. I put away the syrup and butter. When the water boiled I stirred in the oatmeal. I got out the milk and brown sugar. When the oatmeal was done I fixed a bowl and took it out to her.

"Thanks," she said. She sounded apologetic.

"Hey, my pleasure," I said, like I was upbeat.

She stuck her spoon into the oatmeal and pulled out a big dollop. She pulled it toward her mouth. I tried to drink my coffee and watch TV but I was really watching her from the corner of my eye. She got the spoon about an inch from her mouth and held it there. Her mouth opened but closed before she put the spoon in. She tipped the spoon over the bowl and shook out most of the oatmeal. There was a little bit of oatmeal stuck to the spoon. She put that little bit in her mouth and closed her mouth and closed her eyes and swallowed. After a while she exhaled. She opened her eyes and said, "Could I have some more milk on this?"

"Sure," I said. "Coming up." I'd already put in the amount she always liked, so this was not a good sign.

I went to the kitchen and got the milk and brought it out. I held it over the bowl and poured till she said "when." She put the spoon back in and stirred. She stirred for a long time.

After a while I put the milk down and said, "Connie."

Very slowly, she lifted a spoonful to her mouth. I heard her trying to swallow. I took a huge gulp of coffee. I looked at the TV. *Swallow. Swallow. Swallow*, I was thinking. I felt my coffee go down inside me. *Stay. Stay. Stay*, I thought.

She put the spoon down carefully. She sat back against the couch. I could hear her taking deep, even breaths.

I started to count. I got to three.

She said, "Excuse me."

"OK," I said. I wanted her to ask me to help, but she didn't.

I put the oatmeal and everything on the tray and carried it back to the kitchen. I turned the hot water on in the left sink and squirted in some soap. I didn't look into the living room to see her get her cane and stumble up, because she didn't want me to see. I didn't ask her if I could help because she'd made me promise I wouldn't.

I stood over the sink, my back to the hall that went to the bathroom and bedroom. I had the water running loud, but I could hear exactly what was happening because it happened the same way every time: the shuffle of her feet and the thump of her cane down the hall. Then the sound of her opening the bathroom door and the sound of her clicking on the light and fan, and then the sound of the fan and her closing the door. Then there was the sound, behind the door, of her sobbing. I turned the water from hot to cold and the faucet from the soapy sink to the other. And then, because she wanted me to, I turned on the disposal. I scraped the pancakes and egg off the plate. I scooped the oatmeal and milk and sugar from the bowl and pushed them down the disposal.

The water was running and the disposal was loud but not so loud it could cover the sound of her being sick.

This was the food she could not eat. None of this could ease her terrible hunger.

It didn't last long and it wasn't much because it

was only what she had. Her body kept trying to get rid of it. Her body was emptied out till there was nothing.

Then there was the sound of her breathing hard and the sound of the toilet flushing and then, in a few more seconds, the door being opened, the light switching off. Then she walked down the hall to her bedroom, to the bed where she'd had her babies. She walked with a hand against the wall and a hand around her cane and she pulled herself onto the bed and lay down.

I poured a glass of water from the bottle on the counter. I waited, as she'd asked me to, until I heard her calling. I took the water in to her. In her room I heard her breathing hard. I heard, although she said it so quietly you wouldn't understand unless you'd heard it many times before and knew exactly what to listen for, what she was trying to say. What she was trying to say was this: "I'm thirsty."

I held the glass with the straw in my hands. I knelt beside the bed and slipped my arm around her neck. I lifted her head and she opened her mouth. I held the water to her mouth and hoped that she could drink.

THE GIFT OF
MOBILITY

I went to see Ed in the hospice.

This hospice was small and new and comfortable. There were rooms for eight residents. You went to your person's room after the front desk called them and found out if they were up for it.

Ed's room had his TV and his sheets on the bed and his pictures on the wall and some of his knick-knacks I used to dust. It was nice that the room looked like his, like he was going to live there for a while, not just a room people went through.

"Nice place," I said.

"Yeah," he said, "I really like my room."

It was good that he called it "my" room.

I told him he looked good and he said, "Do you really think so?" and I said yeah. He did look OK. In comparison to the other people in the hospice he looked terrific.

Ed started right in talking about the hospice. He said he'd made some friends there. He said he'd made this huge impression the day he moved in. The guys had known he was supposed to come earlier, the first time the hospice called him. They'd put his name up on the door as soon as they took the other guy's name off. But then when Ed didn't show up the guys figured he'd died. So when he did move in later (the guy who had taken the room had only lasted a while), they said, "What a coincidence, another guy named Ed was going to move in earlier but he died," and Ed said, "That's me, I'm that Ed," and they said, "You didn't die?" and Ed said, "No." He told them he'd just turned the room down the first time because he didn't feel like moving in then, and the guys were very impressed. No one had ever turned down a room. So everyone thought Ed was really something, that he'd beat the system. Then they started joking, then hoping, that if Ed could beat the system maybe he could beat the whole thing. Maybe he could be the guy who got out of that place alive.

I hadn't seen Ed for weeks. When I was still at his apartment he'd said his sister was coming to visit him and he wouldn't need, and didn't want, anyone except the nurse to come over. He'd called Margaret and his case manager and said so. But a while after his sister was supposed to be there, the nurse called his case manager and said Ed's place was a wreck—that no sister had ever showed up but Ed hadn't told anyone and he was trying to do everything himself. Ed was a wreck too. Ed's case manager got him back to the top of the waiting list for a room at the hospice. Ed didn't want to go there, but he had to go somewhere.

The first time I went to see him there he seemed different. There was a kind of sharpness about him. He didn't want to talk about his sister or his apartment or anything in his life before. He went on about how "I didn't come here till I was goddamn good and ready. I could have gone somewhere else, but I picked this place. I came here in my own sweet time. Nobody made me."

Right before I left he said, "Why did you come here?"

"To see you," I said.

"You didn't have to?" he asked.

When they moved into the hospice, or even the hospital for a while, they stopped being home care clients. That's what he was referring to.

"I didn't have to, Ed," I said. "I just wanted to see you."

He looked away from me and shrugged his shoulders and said, very quietly, "Oh."

When I left he walked me to the door. I slipped my arm around his waist and he hugged me. He was stiff but he held me a long time. When we were still like that he said, "Will you come again?"

"I'd like to," I said.

"OK," he said.

I went to see him every weekend. The first few weeks he liked it there. He made all these friends. He introduced me to them. I'd never met any friends of his before, he'd never talked about anyone. He said he loved how all his friends at the hospice would sit around and talk and gossip. He said they really understood each other. It was like old guys trading war stories. He said they all smoked like chimneys, the ones who could, even the ones who never smoked before. He laughed. He said, "I mean, like who's going to tell us to quit?"

Sometimes when I called before I went to ask if I could bring anything, he'd say, "Cigarettes?" They all shared them with each other.

It was good to see Ed there. He'd been so depressed before he'd left his apartment. The only people he ever saw were home care aides and medical people and gorgeous perfect TV characters. A lot of people he knew had died, and he said he didn't want to see anyone anymore anyhow. For a while at the hospice he had a lot of energy because of all the other people.

But after he'd been there about a month one of his new friends died. Then the next weekend, two more. They seemed to go like that, in clumps. They were replaced by new people, and the new people were nice, and Ed always tried to be nice to them, but the more he stayed the less he wanted to make friends. He said he didn't like making friends with people when they just died.

Then one time I went there and he was the only

one left from when he first arrived. All the others had died. He didn't like being the oldest person. He said he felt like people were just waiting for him to go, like he'd been in the room he was in too long and had worn out his welcome. "There is a waiting list, after all," he said sarcastically, then sighed and said he didn't really think the people who worked there were waiting for him to die, but he was. He said he felt like he was in a holding tank waiting to die.

He asked if I remembered how he used to wait for the hospice to call and say they had a room for him. I said yeah, I remembered. That was the only thing he ever talked about from before. He said that now he realized that what he'd been waiting for was someone in this room, he didn't call it "my" room, to die.

He said whenever someone died they all talked about them for a day or two but then stopped. There were so many new people all the time you couldn't remember everyone who died. He said, "There won't be anyone left to remember us when we all die."

The next time I went to see him I asked him how he was doing. He snapped, "I've got AIDS. That's how I'm doing." I didn't say anything. He looked up at the ceiling.

I said, "I brought some cigs."
He said, "Thanks."
I got them out to give him. He didn't take them

right away. He was blinking at the ceiling. His eyes were red. His lips were tight. In a few seconds he put out his hand and said, very meekly, "Thank you." He took the cigarettes. The wrapper rustled because his hands were shaking. "I'm sorry I snapped at you," he said.

"That's OK, Ed," I said.

He said he wanted to go outside and have one. They weren't allowed to smoke inside. We went outside and sat at a table under a big sun umbrella. It was a gorgeous day. I started talking to him about what I'd been up to. He used to ask me that kind of thing. He nodded every now and then but didn't say anything. After a while I stopped talking and we just sat there. Later another guy, a new guy I'd never seen, shuffled up. He and Ed did a high five and clutched hands. It was a pretty weak high five. Ed offered the guy a cigarette and he sat down.

I said hi to the guy but Ed didn't introduce us. The guy and Ed started talking about people I didn't know, new people at the hospice. When they stopped talking to light up again, I said, "Well, I think I'll be going."

"Oh," Ed said, suddenly embarrassed. "I'll walk you to the door." He shook his match out and set his cigarette in the ashtray. He stood up and introduced me to the guy. He said to the guy about me, "This is my friend."

We walked to the door. Ed liked being able to do this. A lot of the residents couldn't, so sometimes when their visitors were leaving, Ed would get up and walk them to the door too. It was important to him to be a little different from the really sick guys.

At the door I hugged him goodbye like we always did then. When I was about to take my arms away he squeezed me tighter.

"I'm sorry I haven't been very nice lately," he said into my hair.

"Ed, you've been fine," I said. But I knew what he meant.

He was still holding me, so I couldn't see his face. "I don't like being here anymore," he said. "I wish I could go away."

"I'm sorry, Ed," I said. My cheek was against his chest. I could feel his ribs.

"Everybody here dies," he said.

I squeezed him. I could hear his pulse, his heart. It sounded so normal.

"Remember when the guys used to think Super Ed would beat the system?"

I nodded. "Yeah."

He squeezed me and took a deep breath. His lungs sounded normal too. "All the guys who named me Super Ed are dead."

I could smell his skin. He smelled so clean.

"I told some of the new guys the story," he said,

"but it's different. They aren't the ones who were there—"

Suddenly he loosened away from me and put his hands on my shoulders. "Thank you for coming to see me," he said. "It's meant a lot to me."

It sounded very final the way he said it.

"I like you, Ed. I like to see you."

"*Thank you*," he said again. He was very insistent.

Then, abruptly, he dropped his arms and turned away. I couldn't see his face but he made this gesture with his hands for me to go so I did. I closed the hospice door behind me. I looked through the frosted glass. I could see the shape of him through it. His head was down. His face was in his hands.

The next weekend when I called the hospice and asked for Ed the receptionist said he'd left. I asked when she expected him back, like he'd gone out to see a doc or finally started taking some class at the adult day care, but the woman said, "He's *left*. Gone. He's not a resident anymore."

I felt this thud in my chest. I don't know if I said anything.

Then she explained that Ed had wanted to leave and they had to let him because the hospice was voluntary admission. She said he found a place to move into and they took him there: the Y.

I called the Y, but he wasn't there and no one

remembered him. According to their records he'd left the same day he'd been brought there to check in. They didn't know where he'd gone. I called Margaret, but she was out—she seemed to be out a lot these days—so I talked to Donald, her assistant. He was nice, but UCS hadn't kept track of Ed since he'd gone to the hospice and stopped being a client. I called Ed's case manager, but he was out too, and the guy I talked to told me that because of their confidentiality policy he couldn't pass on information about anyone, he couldn't even tell me if someone was a client. All I could do was leave a message for Ed, if he was a client and if he got in touch with them, that I was trying to reach him. Before I got off the phone I asked if they'd been in touch with Ed's sister, and the guy said, "He has a *sister*?" really surprised. But then he caught himself and said, "Look, I'm truly sorry, but I really can't tell you anything." I said I understood, which I did, but I also didn't know where else to look. There wasn't anyplace for Ed to go.

I went back out to the hospice.

There was a guy on the porch I'd seen before. He was sitting under a huge sun umbrella. He waved to me with his cigarette. He recognized me too. I went over and sat down.

"Ed's not here," he said excitedly.

"I know," I said. "They told me when I called."

"He just left, man," the guy said, all bright-eyed. "He just up and walked right out."

Another guy came out of the day room. "You two talking about Ed?"

"Yeah!" said the first guy, and he raised his hand in a fist.

The second guy sat down and grinned. "Fucking amazing, man," he said. He reached over for the pack of cigarettes on the table.

"He went to the Y?" I asked.

"Who the fuck cares where he went!" the first guy said, lighting the other guy's cigarette. "Ed *walked* outta here on his *own two feet*."

"How was he when he left?" I asked.

The second guy laughed. Not at me, at something bigger. "Vertical," he said, and they both laughed.

"Yo!" said the first guy. Then they both raised their hands and high-fived each other three times, and each time they said, "Yo!" After three they clutched each other's hands and said together, swinging their hands on each syllable, "Su-per-Ed!" like it was a club salute. They were so charged up.

I just sat there. I really felt like a girl.

The second guy leaned over and put his arm around my shoulder. "Hey, don't be sad, honey, we'll all miss him, but Ed—" He chuckled. His eyes were bright. He pulled me close. I felt his body humming.

The other guy let out a wild whoop and laughed and whooped again.

My guy pulled me close and held me tight and whispered in my ear what gave him hope: "Our Ed got outta this friggin' holding tank *alive*."

THE GIFT OF
DEATH

Margaret asked if I could fill in for a few hours on a Saturday afternoon for a new client. The guy had just moved, "reluctantly" she said, into a public housing authority building, and needed to have his things unpacked, maybe some light meals, etc. Margaret read this to me over the phone from the intake form. The guy didn't have a primary caregiver, but he had a friend named Andrew who was helping him settle in. The guy's name was Francis.

This housing authority building had ten floors. I'd been there several times before to see clients. There were seniors and handicapped people living there too, not just PWAs. The building overlooked the freeway, so the rooms with views sounded like traffic and the rooms that didn't sound like traffic faced right up against other buildings.

I was supposed to be there at one. As I was walking up to the door I pulled the piece of paper from my pack that had his apartment number on it. I was just about to buzz when a guy who'd been sitting on the wall smoking a cigarette came up.

"Are you from UCS?" he asked, and I said yes. "To see Francis Martin?" and I said yes again. He said he was Andrew and the apartment buzzer was broken so he'd come down to let me in. He stubbed out his cigarette and we went in. The building smelled like boiled food and dirty laundry. We waited for the elevator. It took forever. There was an old woman in a wheelchair waiting, and a middle-aged guy in a shower cap reading *Soap Opera Digest*. Also a twitchy youngish guy wearing the thickest glasses I'd ever seen in my life. The lenses were completely smudged. He was wearing a Sea World t-shirt with a pair of leaping dolphins. If I'd been by myself I would have taken the stairs, but I didn't want to suggest anything that might be hard on Andrew. You never knew who was sick anymore.

While we were waiting Andrew told me about his friend. Most I already knew from Margaret. Francis had been primary caregiver to a friend of his who had died a while back, and when he started going downhill himself recently, he said he didn't want to fight it, he just wanted to be allowed to die. Andrew said the friend who'd died had had a really painful time of it and Francis didn't want to go through that.

I felt uncomfortable having Andrew tell me all this right there in front of everyone else waiting for the elevator, but they didn't seem to be listening. That kind of story wasn't novel to them. Everyone who lived there had some kind of problem.

Finally the elevator came. There was a slow creak-ing noise, then a thump, then the doors jiggled open. A beautifully dressed woman with her hair up in a bun got off. She was pushing a little grocery cart. When she walked past me I saw the worn threads of her coat. Her coat was smeared and she smelled sweet but underneath she smelled rancid. There was a huge fat man with huge white hands sitting on a bench in the back of the elevator. The buttons on his shirt looked like they were about to pop. The elevator was like a freight elevator, big enough to fit stretchers and wheelchairs in. I hesitated, waiting for the man on the bench to get off, but everyone got on so I did too. The doors closed and you could smell someone. There was a low creak then a jolt. Then this froggy voice. "Hello Anna Weber."

The woman in the wheelchair sighed. "Hello, Roy." Then it said, "Hello James Green," and the guy in the shower cap said, "Yo, Roy." Then it said, "Hello Mark Ullman," and the guy in the glasses whined, "Hi." Then it said, "Hello Andrew O'Donnell," and Andrew said, "Hello, Roy." Then it said to me, "And who are you?"

I turned around to face him. It was the fat guy on the bench speaking. No one else had turned around to say hello to him. They'd just kept watching the eleva-tor floor lights. I started to say something, but then we were on Anna's floor and the elevator stopped and the doors opened and Anna wheeled herself out.

"Goodbye Anna Weber," he said. "Bye, Roy," she said impatiently. Roy looked between us all out into the hall. He looked very intently to see what was happening on that floor; nothing was.

When the doors closed he asked me again, "And who are you?" and I told him my name and he made this spitting sound; it was him giggling. "I know," he said, like I'd just fallen for this incredibly funny joke. Then he said very seriously, "I know you. I've seen you before."

It felt weird to think of this guy watching me from the elevator when I'd been in the building before.

"Who are you here to see today?" he asked. He really did know everyone's business.

"A friend," I said. Because of the confidentiality thing we didn't tell people who we were seeing or for what. It was up to the clients themselves to say what they wanted their neighbors to know.

The elevator still hadn't moved. Andrew punched the Close button. He waited a couple seconds then hit the floor buttons.

Roy looked at Andrew, then back at me. "Is Andrew O'Donnell taking you to see Francis Martin?"

"Yup," said Andrew. He was hitting the floor buttons.

"Francis Martin has AIDS," said Roy.

"Yup," said Andrew again. The elevator creaked.

Then Roy said, "So do Jean Brownworth, Edward Perry, Keisha Williams, Jordan Williams . . . ," and he went through this list.

I looked up at the blinking elevator lights. James and Andrew were looking up at them too. Mark's head was cocked to the right. He wasn't looking at anything. Roy finished his list of "so do's," then went on with a list of "so did's." It was a long list. Andrew kept hitting the floor buttons, and the elevator began to move. By the time Roy finished "so did," we'd gone up two floors.

The elevator stopped, but the doors stayed closed. Andrew sighed. He punched the Open button and the doors opened. But it wasn't anybody's floor so no one got out. Then he punched the Close button and pulled the doors shut. We sat there and he punched the floor buttons and we started to move again.

I felt Roy looking at me. I turned to him. The elevator was making noise, but it sounded very quiet with no one talking. Roy was staring at me. The elevator stopped between floors.

"That's quite a memory you have, Roy," I said.

"Yes, it is," he said without blinking. "I know all the names from Western State Hospital for fourteen years."

"Uh-huh," I said.

"I was at Western State Hospital for fourteen years before I came here." He was staring at me.

"Oh yeah?" I said.

Andrew crossed his arms and closed his eyes and sighed.

"When's this fuckin' box gonna move," said James.

Mark made a noise.

"Before that I was in Pierce County Youth Services Home," Roy said, still staring at me. "I know all the names from there too."

"That's a lot of names," I said.

"I know your name too," he said.

I felt my skin crawl. Andrew held a floor button down. The elevator groaned and started moving up.

"And I'm glad you do, Roy," I said, as brightly as I could. "It's a pleasure to meet you." I put out my hand for him to shake. He looked down at my hand. His eyes were little and piggy. They were gray and watery like an egg at the edges. Suddenly he shot his hand up and took mine and shook it furiously. His hand was wet and soft.

The elevator thumped then stopped and Andrew pushed the Open button and said, "This is our floor."

I started pulling my hand away from Roy, but he wouldn't let go.

"It's nice to meet you, Roy," I said, "but I have to go now."

Andrew was holding the elevator open. It was starting to buzz.

"I have to go now, Roy," I said.

He was still staring at me. Suddenly he blinked

and snatched his hand out of mine. He balled it up in a tight white fist and slapped it down on his thigh.

As the doors were closing behind us I heard him saying goodbye to me and Andrew by our names.

We walked down the hall.

"Roy is our welcome committee," Andrew said.

"I see," I said.

"I guess archivist is more like it." Andrew tried to laugh. "He also does the obits."

I didn't know if I was supposed to laugh. "It's amazing he remembers all the names."

"It's nice someone does," Andrew sighed.

Then we were at Francis's door.

The apartment had the same layout as a lot of them in the building: small kitchen, tiny bathroom, and a main room with a track on the ceiling and floor where you pulled a partition out to make a wall to separate the bedroom. There were boxes on the floor and kitchen counters and in the bathroom. But not many. The guy didn't have much stuff. The main room had a table and two chairs and nothing else. The partition wasn't out. Francis was lying on his side with his arm over his face.

Andrew said I could put the kitchen things away first, then if I had time, the bathroom. He said there was no set way to do the kitchen, just try to be logical because there would be a lot of different home care aides, etc., in and out.

There was a moan. Francis was turning in his sleep.

Andrew said, "Well, I need to get home and get some rest. I'd like to introduce you, but I don't want to wake him."

"That's OK," I said. "I'll tell him who I am when he wakes up."

Andrew said fine and that he'd be back around five. He left his number in case I needed anything.

Andrew left and I started unpacking the kitchen things. I put away plates and glasses and forks. I looked at Francis's stuff and wondered about what kind of life he had, if he cooked a lot or had dinner parties or takeout and fast food. I laid out shelf paper and arranged things. There were cutesy dish towels from Savannah and Williamsburg and "olde time" pictures of colonial houses with recipes on them for Mom's Apple Pie and Country Fried Chicken. There was an old Betty Crocker and an organic cookbook and a book about power eating to help your immune system. There were half-empty cans of protein powder and bottles of vitamins and oils and tinctures and lots of meds. Most of the plates and things didn't match, like he'd gone to Goodwill or garage sales a lot or inherited things from people who'd died. I thought of this stuff going on to other people after he died and how they would have it until they died. All this stuff would outlast everybody.

I heard another moan. I went to the bed. He rolled over and opened his eyes.

"Hi, Francis," I said. "I'm from UCS."

He blinked at me a couple of times. "I know," he said slowly. "I know you."

"I don't think we've met before," I said. Sometimes with dementia they confused you with other people.

But he went on. "I don't remember your name, but I know you." He tried to raise his hand. I took it to shake. "I'm Marty," he said.

But his name was supposed to be Francis, Francis Martin. Then I got it: Marty.

"Hi, Marty." I shook his hand. "Nice to meet you." I told him my name.

"We've met before," he insisted.

"Uh-huh," I said vaguely. There was no point in trying to correct someone with dementia.

He kept looking at me very intently. "I was Carlos's friend," he said.

I was still shaking his hand, not getting it.

"You came to help Carlos once. He said you were nice. He told me you gave him a bath."

He clutched my hand to stop shaking. Then I remembered and I got a horrible chill. My skin prickled.

"Oh—right!" I said. "Marty!" I tried to sound enthusiastic but it was hard because I was remembering that Marty, Carlos's friend, and I couldn't believe this guy was him. That Marty was about thirty, a pear-shaped guy in polyester pants and a short-sleeved shirt. He looked like he still had baby fat on his face, like he almost never shaved. But this Marty was thin, his face was lined. He wasn't horribly skinny, and if you saw him for the first time you might not think he was sick, just trim. But he didn't look thirty. He looked about fifty. I tried to smile like it was nice to run into him again but it was horrifying.

I saw him recognize the look on my face. But he was polite, he tried to make conversation. "So, you're still doing this, huh?"

"Yeah," I said.

"Shit, girl," he laughed. His teeth were brown. "If I were you I'd have moved on ages ago."

I shrugged. I was remembering how he'd apologized when he'd said "damn" when I'd seen him before.

Then he said, "But I'm glad you didn't. It's nice to see you again."

"It's nice to see you again too, Marty," I said, and I meant it then. I felt something when I thought about Marty and Carlos.

Marty started to cough and I helped him sit up and handed him his glass of water from the floor. He took a drink and I rearranged his pillows behind him.

"Thanks," he said. He handed me the water to put back on the floor. There was no bedside table. Some of them tried to get rid of most of their stuff before they died so no one would have to deal with it. Also they liked being able to give special things to friends. Or they had to sell things for money. Or they had to get rid of things in order to fit into the tiny places where they had to move.

"What a dump, huh?" he sighed. "I didn't want to move here, but my old apartment got to be too much for me, and I couldn't find anyone to move in. . . . Andrew's already taking care of Michael . . ."

"Jeez." I shook my head.

"So," he said, "it ain't the Ritz, but I guess it's home." He was trying to sound chirpy. "You meet any of my neighbors on your way up?"

"Yeah," I said. "That elevator takes forever."

He snickered. "You're not kidding. It's gonna be great when there's a fire or something here someday." He rolled his eyes. "I told Andrew he needs to find some patron saint of elevator repair. Andy's a good Catholic boy, you know." He winked at me. I laughed. I was glad we were talking about something else.

"I bet you met Roy, huh?"

"Yeah," I said, "he's something."

"Poor bastard," said Marty. "He's lived here forever. I used to see him in the elevator all the time when I came here before I lived here, to visit friends."

I wondered how many of Marty's friends had died.

"It kind of freaked me out when I was moving in and he told me all the names and put me on the list too," Marty said.

I thought of how strange I felt when Roy told me he knew my name. It was nothing compared to what Marty must have felt.

"In a way it's a kick," Marty said. "I mean, he really knows what's what. But when you think that that's his whole life, that all he's ever done is know all these names, it's pathetic. His whole life has been miserable since day one. Always being shuffled around to 'live'"—he spat the word out—"in these godforsaken places . . . "

"Poor guy," I said.

Marty just sat there staring for a minute. Then he went on. "He'll probably live to be a hundred." He shook his head. "And that, truly, is a tragedy. To have to live when your life is nothing. I mean, he's never lived outside an institution, never had a real home. I bet he's never been in love or been to a nice restaurant or taken a vacation. I bet he's never had anyone give him flowers. I mean, I don't think anybody's ever loved him."

He put his hand on his chest. I got his water and held the glass while he sucked through the straw. He drank slowly then caught his breath. But he wasn't finished.

"And all these old ladies who live here—I bet half

of them don't want to be alive. They've been aban-
doned by their families, or never had families, and
they live on ten measly cents a day and eat cat food
and watch game shows and are lonely. And if they
were ever married they've outlived their husbands by
fifty years and are just waiting to die. I bet if you gave
them a choice, I mean really gave them a choice, if
you said, 'Here, tonight you can go quietly and pain-
lessly and have it over with . . . ' "

He stopped talking and nodded for the water. I
handed him the glass and he drank. When he finished
he said, "I guess you know Carlos died."

In fact I didn't know for sure. But I'd assumed
he'd died. You always assumed all of them died.

"Carlos was in a lot of pain at the end," Marty
said.

"I'm sorry," I said.

"A whole lot of pain," Marty said. "It was criminal
that his docs wouldn't give him something to help
him go. He wanted to. But they had no mercy." Marty
looked through me, then at me. "They wanted to
move him to the hospice but there were never any
rooms. That was fine because he didn't want to go, he
just wanted to die at home." Marty looked up at the
ceiling and blinked. Then he closed his eyes and didn't
say anything.

After a while I said, tentatively, "You were with
him?"

He opened his eyes, then squinted at me. I didn't look away.

"Yes," he said.

He sighed, and when he spoke again his voice was very quiet. "Carlos and I had known each other since we were kids. We were always just friends, you know, we had never had an affair or anything, but we went through everything together. He'd have done anything for me. Anything absolutely. And me for him."

He looked at me again like he was checking me out. "Have you ever had a friend like that?"

"Yes," I said immediately.

He nodded, his eyes still on me. "Carlos was tired of struggling. He was in so much pain."

Marty's mouth got tight.

"I know what you mean," I said.

He took a deep breath and got this look on his face, like when you ask a question you're not sure you want to know the answer to.

"Do you think it can be a relief to die?" he asked.

"Yes, Marty," I said.

He was holding his breath, then he released it. His mouth softened. Then he looked at me so longingly. He wanted me to know.

"I helped him," he said.

"You were a good friend to Carlos," I said.

"I was," he said. "I was merciful. I gave him the gift of death."

THE GIFT OF
SPEECH

When the epidemic started there was a shorter time between when people got sick and when they died. Also when the epidemic started everyone thought it wouldn't last that long because someone would find a cure. So when UCS started they asked you for a six-month commitment because that would usually cover how long your people would stay alive and you could see them through to the end. But the epidemic kept going on. They found meds that could slow the virus or some of the symptoms so people could be alive longer. Then you could be with someone a year or two or even more, you could get really used to being with them. But nobody found a cure so everyone still died. It just took them longer.

Usually they'd be sick but maintaining. Then they'd get a bout of something worse and be hospitalized and you'd think they were going to die but they'd pull through. Then they'd get another bout and you'd think they were really going to die but they didn't again, so then you got to thinking that they would keep pulling through until there was a cure. You'd start thinking they weren't going to die.

After they died you missed them. But also there was a way you missed them before they died because you knew they were going to die. You tried to be careful so it wouldn't get in the way of how you were supposed to be with them, how you wanted to be, but sometimes you couldn't and it was very difficult when they went.

It took the epidemic going on for many years before there were any hospices. First there was one, then another. People could only go there when they had less than six months left to live. The idea was to have somewhere "comfortable" to die. When the hospices opened there was a huge waiting list for the rooms, so you were lucky if you got one. But there was a quick turnover because everyone died so quickly. But the waiting list kept growing because more people got sick.

Rick got a room at the hospice a few weeks after Ed left.

I'd gone over to Rick's the way I did every Tuesday and Thursday morning. I knocked on his door and yelled, "Hey, buddy!" and let myself in. Rick hadn't answered his door himself in a while. I went in and said, "So how's my main man today?"

He was on the couch under his down comforter.

"I got a room," he said quietly.

I knew he meant at the hospice. "Oh," I said. He'd

been waiting for a while, but when you actually got it, it was like getting your sentence.

"I'm glad there's a room for you," I said.

"I'm glad there's a room too." He pulled his comforter up closer under his chin.

I started taking off my jacket.

"You don't have to stay here today," Rick said. "I don't need you to do any work."

He'd never called it "work" before. He'd always called it "help." And when I'd heard him talk on the phone he didn't call me his "home care aide" or "home care worker," he called me my name like I was just someone he knew.

"There's no point in you staying," he said. "My friends from the pagan circle have been planning to help me move when I go to the hospice and they're coming over this afternoon and they can help clean up so you don't have to stay and do any work, you can go." He said it all in one breath.

I took off my jacket and put it over the back of the chair the way I always did. He'd told me before how his pagan friends were going to help him with the move, and that made sense, but I didn't believe he wanted me to go.

"Rick," I said, "I'm not only here to do chores. I like seeing you. I like being around you."

He looked down at the comforter like he was memorizing it. "It's different now," he said. He didn't say anything for a while, then he said the same thing he'd already said except really cheery. "I'm really glad there's a room for me. I'm really lucky to get one."

When I didn't say anything he went on. "It's a nice place. The people who work there are really nice. You've been there?"

"Yeah," I said. But I didn't talk about anybody with anybody else. You weren't supposed to, but I wouldn't anyway. You tried to be only where you were, you tried not to add them up.

"I used to visit all the time," he said. "Even after Barry."

So many of these guys, all their friends were dying too. Like a bunch of ninety-five-year-olds watching their generation end.

I reached for his hands, but he wouldn't let me hold them. He started picking at a thread at the edge of the comforter. After a while he stopped and folded his hands across his chest and looked out the window. I could see the veins in his hands.

"The people who work there are really nice," he said again. He talked about how all the "residents," which was what they called people who went there, had their own rooms and could bring their own stuff from home if they wanted and could watch TV together in the common room if they could with friends from the outside. He mentioned some of the things he wanted to take with him: some prints and cassettes and his boombox, some incense and crystals and stones, his fairy gear. He picked at the thread on the comforter again then repeated the things he wanted to take: his tapes and boombox, etc. Then he stopped talking and looked out the window. A muscle in his jaw was twitching.

"I'm glad you'll have your stuff there, Rick," I said.

"Thank you," he said.

We sat together for a long time, just sitting. Then after a while he said, "Will you miss me?"

I couldn't say it. I didn't want to break apart. I leaned over to pick him up. I put my arms beneath his back and lifted him and held him close. His body was very thin and light, his skin was dry and cool.

I called the hospice a couple days after he went in. The woman on reception transferred me to his room and a woman from his pagan group answered the phone. I asked her how Rick was and she said he was "comfortable." She said he was sleeping and if I wanted to talk to him to try later.

He was asleep a couple other times when I called. Then I stopped calling.

After Rick went into the hospice Margaret suggested I take some time off before I started with someone new. She'd said the same thing after Ed and

I'd said OK, but this time I didn't want to. I didn't want to go see Rick at the hospice. Then she said why didn't I just do subbing for a while. When you're a sub you fill in for different helpers when they can't make it, you don't spend so much time with any one person. So I became a sub except for staying the regular aide for Connie.

I went to a lot of different people's places. I only saw each person once or a few times. They were all different individuals but they were all very sick.

One time Margaret asked me to go to this guy whose old aide, a guy named Roger, had recently moved to Portland for a job. I'd never met Roger because I'd stopped going to the monthly meetings— they had monthly meetings so you could discuss things about work and your "feelings," but Margaret let me get away with skipping them. Anyway, Margaret was looking for someone to be this guy's regular aide, and until then he was just having subs. Someone had to be with him all the time. He slept a lot and had some incontinence and basically would be pretty standard—cleaning, light meals, being there in case. I'd need to be there till five, when another aide would come.

Margaret was giving me the address. "It's an apartment building, Monroe Court. It's on—"

"I know where it is," I interrupted her. I'd been there before for somebody.

She paused. "You OK?"

"Sure," I said.

"I can try to find someone else," she said. "Or Donald can."

Margaret seemed to be sloughing a lot of her work off onto Donald these days. I didn't get it. I wasn't going to pass my work on to someone else.

"I'm OK," I said. "Who is he?"

She told me the guy's name, Mike, and I went.

Monroe Court is a big apartment building, so I didn't expect this guy Mike to know the other guy I'd seen there before. Also, it was on the Hill, so if I'd said, "Do you know a guy who used to live here who had AIDS?" I could have been referring to any number of guys.

Mike lived on the seventh floor. I took the elevator up, then walked down the hall to his apartment. It was an outside room, it would have a great view. I knocked, and the other aide came out in the hall and told me that Mike was asleep and what he'd had to eat and then he left. I went in. The curtains were drawn so you couldn't see out. The heat was on and it was stuffy. The plants were turning yellow. It was a one-room studio.

Mike opened his eyes when I came in. I went over to his bed. It was a hideaway, and I bet it was never up anymore. I introduced myself. He mumbled something and closed his eyes again and went back to sleep. Things were pretty clean but I cleaned anyway. I did the kitchen alcove. I kept looking into the bedroom section every so often to see if he was awake or wanted anything. I worked quietly, didn't turn on the radio or run the vacuum. There was just the sound of me getting water in the bucket and washing the cupboards and cabinets and floors and taking gloves on and off and washing my hands.

Mike woke up. He didn't need changing. I made him a protein smoothie and sat with him and helped him drink it. He said thanks for the smoothie and that it tasted great. "As good as Roger's," he said, "only different." He asked me if I could come again. I said I didn't know, that it depended on scheduling, which was a lie. Margaret was trying to find a regular helper for Mike, and I could be it, but I didn't want to be anybody else's regular person except for staying with Connie.

Mike said he hoped he could get a permanent person. He said all the subs were very nice but it was hard having so many different people in and out all the time. He said he hoped he'd get someone like Roger. Mike said he was glad that Roger got a job in Portland but he was sorry he had to move. He said Roger was a great guy. He said he'd been with him for two and a half years, two years and five months to be exact. Mike said, "I miss Roger."

"Uh-huh," I said, the way you do when you're only half listening. Then suddenly I said, "He misses you too, Mike."

"Do you know Roger?" Mike asked, surprised and happy.

"Yes," I lied. "We have these monthly meetings . . . " I took Mike's hands. "You're very important to Roger. He's really glad he got to know you and spend time with you. He really thinks of you a lot."

His face lit up. "Really?"

"Yeah," I said. "He was sorry he didn't get to tell you in words himself before he had to go to Portland, but you're a really important friend to him."

Mike was smiling. "He is to me too," he said. I think he wanted to say more but this was more than he was used to talking. In a few minutes he was asleep again.

Another aide came at five. She actually was someone I recognized from one of the meetings I'd gone to way back when, but I didn't know her. I brought her in and woke Mike and introduced them. She was new to him too.

I called the hospice when I got home. The receptionist transferred me to Rick's room. A woman answered. I asked how Rick was and if he was having any visitors. She said they were trying to keep him "comfortable." I had begun to hate hearing that word.

What it really meant was that it was hopeless. There was always someone with Rick from his pagan circle, so he was never alone, but he didn't have many visitors. She said he was asleep but she'd ask him when he woke up if he wanted me to visit and she'd call me back. She told me he'd stopped his meds and was only on morphine.

The next day she called me and said I could visit Rick. She said he drifted in and out and you never knew how he'd be so I should just come anytime and call from the front desk to see how he was right then.

I went over that evening after I'd subbed at some other people's places. I waited at the desk while they called his room to see if whoever was with him said I should come in. The person said come in.

I hadn't been to the hospice in a while, I'd stopped going after Ed, but it was mostly the same. The common rooms were all the same. The only difference was different names on the residents' doors.

I knocked on Rick's door softly. A woman opened it. She was wearing one of the necklaces Rick made for his friends. He'd made one for me the year before. She introduced herself and took my hand and brought me in. For a second it seemed like I was there to visit her but then she said she would go out for a bit and gestured to a chair beside the bed where I could sit. She was gone so quickly and I was alone with Rick.

I sat by the bed. It was higher than his bed at home. He was sitting up under his comforter and moon-and-stars quilt. I looked at him, then away. He looked awful. I looked around the room at his things. The curtains were closed but someone had lit candles so it was between light and dark. His incense was going, it smelled like outdoors and church. There was chime music on the boombox. On the dresser there were some of his shells and stones and his St. Francis and his wand. I remembered dusting and straightening his things and asking him about them and him telling me. There were some crystals on his bedside table. There were no meds because he was trying to let himself die.

I looked at him. I was glad it was dim. His eyes were open, his left more than his right. Both were rimmed with wet and looked sunk in his head and they were both staring. They were still, like they were only eyes but not his. His cheeks were hollow and his mouth was slightly open and I could hear air going in and out. He was so thin. It was like there was just his skin but nothing else. There was hair on his face. I'd never seen him with a beard, but they'd stopped shaving him.

"Hi, Rick," I said.

He didn't say anything or turn his head. He didn't blink but then he did. I didn't know if he knew I was there or if he was just blinking. I took his hand. It was limp and hot. It didn't move. I reached across the bed and got the other hand in my other hand and held them all together. I held them together like praying hands.

I looked and tried to remember him. I closed my eyes. I thought some words inside myself I would have said to him.

But then I felt bad to have given up on him so I started talking out loud. I whispered at first. It felt odd to talk out loud to myself, and I didn't want anyone else to hear me. But then I didn't want Rick not to hear me if he could so I spoke louder, like a normal conversation.

I told him how nice his room looked, so like him with all his stuff. I said I was glad he was being so well looked after by the hospice people and his pagan circle friends. I told him what I'd been up to like we used to talk when I went to his place. I told him about this cat I adopted.

Rick loved cats. He'd wanted to adopt one that was hanging around his place, but everyone said he could get sicker from the cat, but he said he didn't care. But then he decided not to keep the cat and called everyone he knew till he found someone who could take it. He'd decided he didn't want to keep the cat, then have it miss him and not have a dad after he died.

I'd stopped talking. I was still holding his hands. I

squeezed them and opened my eyes and looked at him. His eyes were still open and looking ahead and his mouth was still open too. He looked exactly the same.

I told Rick I was really glad my new apartment manager said I could have a cat and that my cat had terrible manners because he was so spoiled that he ate off my plate when I got a cinnamon roll from the Hostess, that they were his favorite. Then my mouth stopped moving.

My mouth was dry. I swallowed. "Rick," I said. I stroked his hands. "Rick." I couldn't say anything else. It was quiet for a while.

Then I saw his lips twitch.

"Rick?" I said again.

His mouth opened. It closed, then opened again, and a sound came out.

"What?" I said.

After a few seconds there was the same sound again: "Ngmushu."

I still couldn't understand. "What?" I said again.

His mouth twitched again but there was no sound.

I leaned up close to him. I could smell our sweat. I put my face in front of his so our eyes were looking right into each other. I looked into his eyes and saw: he was still in there.

"Say it again, Rick," I said. "I'm listening."

His lips twitched again and I listened hard. He

said it slow, like I was a beginner at the language: "Ng-mu-shoo."

When it came out that last time I understood. And when I understood I said it back, I said, "I miss you too."

THE GIFT OF
SIGHT

This guy was the scariest to look at. This guy really looked like the plague. Margaret had said the only special thing I'd need to do was put his salve on him. The salve was thick, opaque, yellowish jelly. It came in a big, wide-mouthed plastic jar. It didn't smell like anything. The first time I went there and opened the jar I saw the tracks of someone else's fingers where they'd gone in to get the salve. I don't know why it frightened me so much, but it did. I was afraid to touch him. I was afraid to look at him.

His sores were dark purple and about the size of quarters. The edges of them were yellow and his skin was dark brown. The sores weren't running or oozing or scabs because they always had this salve on them. I was allowed to put on the salve even though I wasn't allowed to give meds because this salve wasn't really a med so much as something just to comfort: it couldn't heal anything.

I don't know if the sores were itchy or hot or how exactly they felt bad to him but I didn't ask. I hadn't been scared to ask about anything before, nurses or docs or Margaret or the guys themselves. The guys especially liked to explain things. They liked that I asked and that they could tell me what they knew. They'd all become experts.

The first time I put the salve on I didn't know if the temperature of it would be uncomfortable, like when massage oil, if it isn't skin temperature, feels so cold that you can't feel the good. I wanted to ask him, but I couldn't. I couldn't say anything out loud about the sores.

I changed gloves several times when I was doing the salve because my gloves got coated with it, and also with his hair, which was very tight and curly and fell out easily, and with flecks or patches of skin. I think he felt embarrassed to have it done except it would have been worse not to have it done.

The first time I went there, his niece, who'd moved in from her dorm to live in his apartment with him, let me in. She showed me around, though there wasn't much to show, the apartment was small. She told me he'd want his dinner but that he could tell me. He could still do that. The niece went out. She was going to get out for a couple of hours to do some errands.

When I asked him what he'd like me to do he said could he have some salve.

"Sure," I said. I pulled the sheet down part way. The sores were all over him. I don't know why the sight of him frightened me but it did. I hadn't felt frightened that way before and I didn't want him to see it in my face, I didn't want him to feel ashamed about how he looked.

Maybe it was seeing it so present, so visible, on the outside, and all the time, not something you could pretend for a while you didn't have, or something that people who only saw you for a while might not see, like chronic diarrhea or the vomits. How he looked was very sick, he looked like he had the plague.

I started with his hands and arms. Then he said, "Could you do my torso, please?"

He said it so normal and evenly, like it was an ordinary task. I tried to think of it as that kind of task, like sweeping the dining room or checking the mail, not something growing on him from his sickness.

I was ashamed of how I thought, of how I tried to think myself away from the terrible sight of his sickness.

I did his torso and his legs and feet. I turned him over and did his back and sides. I did his neck. He didn't have them on his face. I changed his sheets around him. He was breathing hard. The sheets were covered all over with salve. His niece had told me they needed changing twice a day. It took a while for his breathing to calm down.

After a while he wanted his dinner and told me where everything was. It was easy—a microwave frozen dinner and a glass of cranberry juice. Cranberry juice is a good source of potassium. The dinner was roast beef and potatoes and peas and apple pie. I pulled the bed tray over to him and helped him sit up a little. He wanted to feed himself. I put the fork in his hand. He could do almost OK with the potatoes, but the peas were hard to keep on the fork and the roast beef was hard to spear. He asked me to help and I fed him. I lifted the back of his head and put the fork to his mouth. I held the glass up close to him and he drank through the straw. The muscles moving in his neck when he drank looked strong. That was good to see. I got him a second glass. He said, "Thank you."

He was sweaty when he finished. I sponged him clean and put on more salve. He fell asleep. He was breathing fairly evenly. When his niece came home I told her how it had gone and she said thanks and asked if I could come again.

That was Sunday. I could only do weekends for them, so I didn't see him again till the next Saturday. When Margaret had asked me if I could do weekends I'd said yeah, but only for a while, because I wanted to go to San Francisco at the end of next month, and Margaret had said, "They won't need you more than that." Meaning, this guy was not going to last that long.

The next Saturday his niece let me in again and went out, and I said to him, "How about some salve?" like it didn't bother me at all. I'd thought about the sores all week long, about how they looked and how it frightened me. But I'd worked myself up to acting like it didn't bother me.

"Thank you," he said.

I started putting salve on him. I was not going to think about other things. I was going to stay with him even in my mind. I asked him about this painting above the bed. It was on cloth and very beautiful. He turned his head a little to look up at it. He told me he got it in Africa. There were two others, smaller, on the opposite wall. I asked him what had taken him there, and he told me about his teaching. Then how his family, especially his mother—he nodded over at the mantelpiece—had thought it was the greatest, his going back to Africa, it was like back home, and that she'd even talked about going to visit him there.

Part of it felt good, like a normal conversation you'd have with someone you met at a party or with a new neighbor. But also it was like there were four different people there. The two people having the normal conversation and the person touching the body with the salve and the person with the body with the sores.

He said he'd like to have lived there longer but it was better to come back to the States. This was a reference to his getting sick. I was glad to hear him talk about his work and how much he loved it, but part of me was thinking, "But that's where you got sick. That's where you had to come back from to die." I hated myself for thinking that. But I also kept telling myself that even if I wasn't feeling or thinking the right things, at least he was getting fed, at least he was getting his sheets changed, at least his kitchen was getting cleaned, at least his body was getting salve.

When he slept again I went to look at the photo on the mantel. It was of him and his mother. He was in a suit, his arm was around her, his springy black hair was plastered down.

He woke when his niece came back. He looked up and said, "It was nice to talk with you. Are you coming back tomorrow?"

"Next Saturday," I said.

"Thank you for asking about my work," he said. "I want to hear about you next time." He was very polite.

"OK," I said. I still had my gloves on. I shook his hand. "I'll tell you next week."

The next Saturday when I got there, the niece was dressed up. She was on her way to the airport to pick up her grandmother. He had suddenly gotten worse.

He was on oxygen. The tank was by the bed. The tubes were up his nose. His skin was damp. The sores were the same.

I asked the niece what she'd like me to do, and she said he could use his salve and clean sheets but nothing else. "He's not really eating much anymore," she said. She shrugged her shoulders and pointed at the couch. "There's some magazines if you want to read," she said.

"OK," I said. "Drive safe."

"Thanks." She tried to smile. She looked so old. She was a sophomore at the university. She turned to him on the bed. "I'm going to pick up Grandma at the airport. We'll be back in a couple hours."

When she left I washed my hands and put on my gloves and went over and sat next to the bed. I said, "Hi." His eyes moved but he didn't say anything. I started in on the salve. While I did it I told him about what I'd been up to that week, about a movie I'd gone to and hiking with Chris and a new string game I taught my cat. I could tell he was listening, and I believed he remembered he'd asked me to tell him about myself the weekend before and that I'd said I would.

I could hear the oxygen going in and out of him through the tubes when he breathed. The tubes were thin plastic, a light greenish color. The nose clip that held them in was white plastic. I was careful around the tubes when I did the salve on his shoulders and neck, and very careful too when I changed the sheets.

He was breathing hard after the salve and bed change. I put my hand on his arm until his breathing calmed down. Then I said, "You want some juice? I'll bring some over and see if you want some."

I washed my hands and put on new gloves and

poured some cranberry juice in a cup and got a little teaspoon. I put them on the bedside table and sat by the bed.

"Here's some cranberry juice," I said. "Do you want some?"

His eyes were open but cloudy-looking. It took him a few seconds, then he made this noise. I didn't know if it was yes or no or nothing.

"Can you blink once for 'yes' if you want some juice?" I said.

He looked at me. After a few seconds he opened his mouth. His lips were dry. It took him a while to figure it out. Then he blinked and held his eyes closed. I knew he meant yes.

"OK," I said. "Good. I'm going to put some juice in the spoon and bring it to your mouth so you can drink it."

I dipped the spoon in the juice. It was so tiny, this little drop of clear pink juice. As I moved the spoon toward his mouth I kept my hand on his forearm and said, "I'm bringing the juice to your mouth now. It's near your lips now. OK. Here it is."

I heard the click of the bottom of the spoon on his lower teeth. I tipped the spoon in his mouth and he closed his lips and swallowed.

"Good," I said, "that's good. You want some more?"

He blinked.

"OK," I said. I got another spoonful of juice and

brought it toward his mouth. "OK, here comes some more juice." His lips moved like he was trying to suck. I put the spoon in and turned it over, and he swallowed.

"You're doing great," I said, "really great."

He blinked.

I fed him six spoonfuls, but on the sixth one his throat made a gurgling noise and some of it came back out. He opened his mouth in a big frightened O and made this high whine. I was afraid he'd choke. I put my hand on his chest as if I could smooth the passage. It was less than half a glass.

"It's OK," I said. "You're gonna be OK. Just try to breathe."

He opened and closed his eyes really fast.

"It's all right," I said. "You're all right. Just give it a second."

I held my hand on his chest until he'd calmed down. After a while he blinked: OK.

I wiped the juice from around his face and the top of his chest. I moved the oxygen clip in his nose back from where it had shifted.

"You OK now?"

He blinked.

"Good, " I said. "I'll be back in a second."

I went to the bathroom and cleaned up. I changed my gloves. When I went back his eyes were closed. He was breathing evenly. I put his hand on my arm. His pulse was even.

I went to the kitchen to see if there was any cleaning I could do. Everything was spotless. The niece had been keeping busy.

I looked at the clock. They were probably driving back now. They were going to see him soon.

I went to the bathroom and found a comb. I sat by the bed. In a few seconds he opened his eyes and looked at me.

"How about if I comb your hair?" I said.

He took a few seconds to understand, then he blinked.

I put one hand on his cheek and combed his hair with the other. I combed it very slowly.

His hair was springy and damp with sweat. I combed it, then patted it down with my hand. When I put my hand on his head he made a noise.

"Keith?" I said.

His eyes moved. His eyes were watery and thick. He was trying too hard to focus, the way a baby does when it opens its eyes for the first time.

The skin of his face looked very thin. Then luminous, like light was there. There was the sight of something radiant.

He tried to open his mouth but couldn't. He closed his eyes.

I leaned over the bed and took him in my arms. I held him as tenderly as I could.

"Keith," I said, "your mother is coming. You'll see

your mother soon," I said, "you'll see your mother soon."

I held him and told him again and again. I held him until his mother arrived.

Then I put him in her arms.

THE GIFT OF HOPE

I f you're with a client when they die you have to
go into the office and fill out paperwork about it.
They won't let you phone or mail it in because
they want you in the office so they can check out how
you're doing. It's called "outtake."

Keith died on Saturday so I should have gone into
the office on Monday but I said I couldn't get away
from Connie's. It was late to find a sub and besides
Connie and Joe wanted me, not someone else. In fact
they wanted me to be there more because Connie
was going downhill. I called Margaret on Tuesday but
she was out so I talked to Donald and asked him
about getting authorization to do more hours at
Connie's. A client could only get so many hours from
a home health care aide, which is what I officially
was for Connie, but they could get more, or different,
hours from a respite aide. Respite was a different
program from home care. In respite the client wasn't
the PWA but the PWA's primary caregiver, usually
someone in the family like a spouse or lover or par-
ent or kid. Joe was taking off work and spending lots
of time with Connie. He was her primary caregiver.
Respite aides were supposed to just be there in the

house with the PWA so the primary caregiver could get away for a while—i.e., get "respite" from caring for their dying person. Respite wasn't primarily a chore service, so respite aides weren't technically supposed to do big house cleaning, just little meals and personal assistance. All the programs had very specific job descriptions for funding. The other programs were the buddy program, which was volunteer, and the home hospice program and the food bank and home meals. When UCS started, a couple of guys just organized it out of their house and it was all volunteer. But over the years it grew, got an office, then a bigger office, and developed all these different programs and got funding, etc. It was still all for PWAs, but people had been talking about expanding it to help other disabled people too.

Anyway, I had the time to spend with Connie because I wasn't working with anyone else anymore. After Keith I stopped subbing. I wasn't consciously thinking about quitting, but I was acting like it. But I would have felt bad to quit because it would be, for me, like giving up. Although in some ways I think I already had.

So I was on the phone with Donald from Connie's about Connie and Joe wanting me to be there more and Donald said for me to plan to help them out "as long as they needed," meaning until Connie died. Donald said that Joe should call and request it and that Donald and Connie's caseworker would work something out about me doing respite. Then Donald said, "Wait a minute."

I could hear papers rustling on his desk over the phone. "You haven't come in to do the outtake on Keith Williams yet, have you?" He must have been looking at Margaret's files.

"Not yet," I said. I had begun to hate doing outtakes. I'd told Margaret at our last one that they made me feel hopeless.

"Well, I'll tell you what," Donald said. "Come in to the office tomorrow and we'll do the outtake, and by then I'll have talked to Joe and the caseworker and have the authorization for the additional respite hours with Connie and Joe."

"OK," I said, "except Wednesday is Connie's nurse's short day, so I can't make it till after six or so . . ." Which was an hour after Donald and everybody was supposed to leave the office. "Thursday?" I said.

"OK," he said. "Can you make it at four?"

"Yeah," I said. Then, "Will I be doing the outtake with you or Margaret?"

He paused. "Me."

"OK," I said. "Great." I didn't want him to think I didn't want to do it with him instead of Margaret, but I didn't. I'd only ever done outtakes with Margaret.

Then Donald said, "You haven't read the newsletter, have you?"

"Uh, no." I'd stopped reading them a while ago. You were supposed to pick them up at the office when you dropped off your hours or whatever. The newsletters were monthly and had reports about what had been discussed at the previous monthly meeting, suggestions about solving common problems with clients, office news about who was coming and going, and things that were supposed to be light and funny. After a while they'd all begun to seem the same to me and I stopped reading them. Just like I'd stopped going to the monthly meetings.

"Margaret's quitting," Donald said. "The meeting on Thursday is also a goodbye thing for her. You should be there."

"Sure," I said, startled. There was a huge turnover in aides, which made someone like me who'd been there a couple of years a real old-timer, but supervisors tended to stay a long time, and Margaret had been there forever. "Where's she going?" I asked, meaning, where was her new job or where was her family moving.

"She's staying in town," Donald said. But nothing else. Then I heard him take a deep breath on the other end of the line and he said, "She's sick."

"What?" I asked, but he didn't say anything. When he didn't say it, I knew what it was. "Oh god," I said. "Oh my god." All of a sudden my face felt hot. "I'm sorry, Donald, I had no idea—"

"We're all sorry," he said. He sounded so sad. He'd been Margaret's assistant since he'd been there. She'd trained him about everything.

We didn't say anything for a few seconds. Then I said, "I'll see you at the office at four on Thursday," and we got off the phone.

I put the phone down. Suddenly I had this picture—it wasn't a memory, it wasn't something I'd seen, because I hadn't been there, he'd been all alone—of Rick getting the call from the hospice about them having the room. Then I thought of Ed getting the call. Then of both of them further back, before I knew them, when their doctors had told them how they had tested or what their T-cells were. I tried to imagine Margaret finding out except I couldn't. I couldn't conceive of her being sick.

I went back into Connie's room and said to her, like everything was fine, "UCS can take care of it. I can be here as much as you guys want."

Connie's face lit up. "Oh, I'm so glad!" She sounded so happy. She opened her arms and said, "Come give me a hug!"

I held her longer than usual. I kept holding her and couldn't let go. When she felt me holding her like that she started to stroke my hair. Her hands were thin but stronger than I thought. She said, she sounded so comforting, "Honey, what's wrong? What's wrong? Can you tell me?"

My face was on her shoulder. Her nightie was wet with my tears. I said, "I just found out someone I know is sick."

She held me tighter and said, "Oh, honey, I'm sorry."

I felt the bones of her chest and neck and how thin the disease had made her. But she also felt strong and soft to me. She kept on saying, "Oh, honey, I'm sorry. Poor baby, I'm sorry."

She said it so sweet and comforting. She said it as if she wasn't sick. She still made room to care about somebody else.

I went into the UCS office on Thursday. The office Margaret and Donald and the other supervisors shared was at the end of the hall. Their desks were separated by partitions but you could see and hear around them. On my way to Donald's desk I stopped by Margaret's. I peeked around the partition. The desk was half empty. A bunch of notebooks and file folders were spread around. There were dust marks from where her plants and her bowl of seashells and her pictures of her husband and kids and her box of wind-up toys had been. Half the bookshelves were empty. Her big notebooks and her huge fat files were in stacks on the floor and in cardboard boxes, but Margaret wasn't there.

I went back to Donald's cubicle and knocked on

his partition. He looked up and we said hi and he cleared a pile of papers off the chair by his desk. His office was a mess too. I sat down. The phone rang in another cubicle, and somebody picked it up and started talking. I was glad there was another voice.

"Well," I said, "I started filling out some of the outtake on Keith Williams." I didn't even say, "How's it going?"

"Right," Donald said, and started rooting around the floor for a file. I recognized some of the stuff on the floor from Margaret's desk.

I pushed out a clear space on the desk and put my papers down.

When Donald got up from the floor, I said, like it was a prepared statement, "There was an Advance Directive. The client had a living will. He didn't want 911 or CPR so it was only me with him."

Donald nodded. He had copies of Keith's living will and Advance Directive in his file. Donald didn't write anything down on the outtake.

I was saying the kinds of things you were usually asked on outtake. I was just saying them.

"And, well, I mean, his actual, the actual death wasn't that bad." I didn't want to say his name any-more. "The client was pretty comfortable. And his mother and niece were there almost immediately."

Donald was looking at me. I looked away.

"And I hadn't worked that closely with—the client. I was just a weekend sub for a while."

"I'm glad it was relatively comfortable," said Donald quietly.

"Yeah." I shut my mouth. I was remembering, I was feeling again, the weight of Keith's body against me, how heavy his body had felt when I handed him to his mother. I was remembering how his mother had looked, her eyes were black and dark and sad, her eyes were tearless, and I remembered the dryness of her skin against mine when I gave her boy to her. I was thinking, at least he was still warm, at least she could still feel his body's warmth. I remembered the lightness and the coolness of the air against my skin when I had stopped holding the body.

I sat at Donald's desk and looked down at my hands.

He reached out for my outtake papers, and I gave them to him. It was the shortest outtake I'd ever done.

"I'll finish this later," he mumbled, and stuck the papers in a file.

Then, like I was going through a meeting agenda, I said, "How about the authorization for some respite hours for Connie and Joe Lindstrom?"

I think he heard it in my voice. "That's fine," he sighed. He dug around for another file and found the paper and gave me a copy. That was the end of my agenda. Then I felt nervous.

Donald said, "You stopped by Margaret's desk when you came in."

I couldn't tell if it was a statement or a question, or if he'd heard me there or just knew.

"Yeah," I said.

"I'm going to miss her," he said.

"Yeah," I said, "me too."

He put his hand on my shoulder and said, "Thanks for coming in. We'll see you tonight?"

I said yeah and we said goodbye and I left.

It was about five. I went home to feed my cat and hang out with him for a while. There was going to be pizza at the meeting so I didn't eat anything. After a while I picked myself up and made myself go for a walk by the lake. I walked around for a while.

When you find out someone you know is sick it's different from someone you know because they are sick. When you find out about someone you're surprised about, someone you hadn't ever thought would get it, it's different from someone you thought would get it. It shouldn't be that way but it is. Everyone who gets it didn't have it once, everyone who gets it is a loss.

Because I hadn't been to a meeting in a while I got lost so I was late. I slipped in the open front door and threw my jacket in the guest room and took off my shoes—the guy whose house the meetings were in had nice carpet, so no one was supposed to wear shoes—and went down the hall to the living room. It was packed. Everyone was sitting, lots of people on the floor. I huddled down behind some people in the hallway. I could just see into the living room. Donald was saying, "Thanks, Margaret," and some people were sniffing. I'd missed whatever Margaret had said.

Donald cleared his throat. "You're all familiar with how much Margaret has done for the organization over the years. One of her most important contributions is a very recent one she's been working on recently."

Donald had been an incredibly dedicated aide and a great assistant supervisor, but this was his first time to chair a meeting.

"I know that one of the accomplishments she is most happy about is a new development that will expand some of our current programs to help people disabled not only by AIDS but by other things as well. One of the things the epidemic has done for a lot of us is expose us to how many people need the kind of help we can provide them. So I'm really glad we'll be offering our home care chore services and home meals and the respite program to a wider community. And the real champion of this development has been Margaret, she's been pushing for this expansion for a long time. So thanks again, Margaret. And congratulations." Donald began to clap and so did everyone. People started standing up and clapping, giving Margaret a standing ovation.

When I stood up I could see better. Margaret was sitting on the couch looking out at everyone, smiling and nodding thanks. A guy who had been sitting on the floor in front of her stood up and moved to the side of the couch, out of her way, and clapped too. I recognized him from the photo on her desk. It was David, her husband. Everyone was clapping. I looked around the room. We were clapping for Margaret and the new program and other people too. Margaret wasn't the only person in the room who was sick.

After a couple of minutes Margaret shouted, "OK! OK!" then joked, like the meeting had gotten out of hand, "Order! Order!" and people stopped clapping and sat back down. There was a lot of sniffling. When it was quiet again Margaret elbowed Donald in the ribs and Donald said, "Oh—uh—so." He cleared his throat and asked, "So. Does anyone have some issues with clients they'd like to talk about?" He was opening the discussion period of the meeting the way Margaret used to. Usually people jumped in with things, but no one did then. Margaret drew her shoulders up and said, "Todd, maybe you could begin with telling us what's been going on with your client you were telling me about last week."

I couldn't see Todd, but I heard him from the floor. He told about some client's housemates who wanted him to do things for the whole house, like other guys' laundry and mowing the lawn, etc., which obviously was not what he was there to do. Todd was a nice guy. He used to be the morning person for Ed when I was doing afternoons. After Todd explained the situation, someone else said the same thing had happened to them too and told what they'd done and gave Todd some tips. When they'd figured something out it was quiet. Then Donald said, "Anyone else?" and eventually another guy, his voice sounded very young, said he was afraid he'd hurt his client, like drop him or something, and he just felt nervous, so people talked about that. Then a woman—I recognized Li-Li's voice—talked about trying to figure out if this one client of hers was having dementia or was just being a picky bastard. Li-Li was great. I'd met her at one of these meetings when she started at UCS. Also, she had subbed for Carlos a few times.

I looked around the room and thought of why a lot of the people were there. I knew from things they'd said that Todd was gay, Li-Li wanted to go to med school, Beth's granddaughter had it, Donald's brother was sick, Denise's husband had died of it. Everyone had someone.

I looked up at Donald and Margaret on the couch. They were watching whoever was talking, and nodding, encouraging, trying to draw the person out. There was a third guy on the couch too. At first I didn't recognize him, but then I saw it was Buzz, only with a different hairdo. He had been one of the first people at UCS, then a supervisor, but he'd quit about a year ago. I figured he'd come to the meeting for Margaret's going away.

Buzz was a friend of Henry Brookman, the guy who started UCS back in the eighties. Henry had died in '85. Buzz's boyfriend had died back in the early days too.

Someone finished talking, and Donald asked if anyone else had anything else to bring up. No one did and it felt awkward, then Denise said, "Well, I guess I do," and started off in this really serious, mellow New Age voice about "a difficult issue" with a client who only wanted to eat bad food, like real junk. Denise kept a totally straight face as she was going on about Cheetos and Twinkies and Diet Cherry Coke and cake frosting in the can and double-stuffed mint fake Oreos. She was really getting into the details, and people were starting to laugh, then make gross-out noises or *mmmm!* noises. Then people were really cutting up, shouting out other horrible foods to add to the list—pork rinds, pudding cups, imitation jalapeño-flavored Cheez Whiz, etc. Everyone was going to town, even Donald. But then he brought it back to a real point about how much say did we have in what our clients ate and how much was their personal choice. ("Personal choice" was one of the phrases we heard a lot at orientation.) The bottom line, we were reminded, was that we could suggest things but we were only there to aid them, not order them around, so the decision was up to them.

So everyone was getting punchy. When we got through with the food thing—Denise had managed to keep a straight face throughout, she was amazing—no one else brought up anything else to discuss. Then Margaret said, "So, what about some pizza?" and everybody laughed, the timing was so perfect. Donald jumped up and said, "Great idea," and bustled into the kitchen to get the pizza out of the oven. David, Margaret's husband, went with him. Margaret sat on the couch a few moments, then pushed her hands down on the couch to give herself an extra push up. She looked tan. Some of the meds made people look tan.

Margaret went into the dining room where they were bringing the pizza out. There was a folding chair by a cooler on the floor and she sat down and grabbed David on his way back into the kitchen and they started doing the drinks. People went over to the table for their pizza, and when you wanted a drink you went over to Margaret and she grabbed a bottle of ginger beer from the cooler, pulled it up out of the ice, handed it to David and he aimed it at the trash can and popped the top off into the trash and handed the open bottle to you. It seemed like they did that kind of kidding around together a lot. Everyone went over to get a drink and say something to them.

I went over and Margaret said, "Hey, old-timer," and I said, "Hey, Margaret."

She introduced me and David. She said, about me, "We go all the way back to Uncle Chan's together."

Uncle Chan's was this divey Chinese restaurant where UCS rented the upstairs for their first office outside of Henry Brookman's house. Uncle Chan's was very cheap and very, incredibly, grungy. Rips in the carpet, unidentifiable food smells from long ago, totally kitsch but serious light fixtures, etc. I'd started being a home care aide for UCS just before they moved from Uncle Chan's to the big office.

"That Uncle Chan's was some place," said David.

"It had character," Margaret and I said together. We all laughed.

"So you've been here a long time?" David asked. He seemed like a nice guy.

"Yeah," I said.

"You've been here *forever*," Margaret laughed.

But I hadn't been. I hadn't been there as long as some people. Like her.

A guy next to David started talking to him.

Margaret leaned back in her chair and said, "You're not going to try to do this forever, are you?"

"Actually," I said, "I'm thinking about quitting." It was the first time I'd said it, or even thought it consciously.

"That's great," Margaret said before I could make excuses. She knew me well. "It'd be great for you to do something else. And you can always come back and be a perennial."

Perennials were people who worked for UCS for a while, then did something else, then came back for a while, then did something else, back and forth. Margaret had always encouraged people to take off if they needed to. People handled things differently. I could become a perennial; I had all the time in the world.

"Hey," Margaret said, "Buzz is here tonight," and nodded over at him. "He just got in from New York. He loves it there."

"Yeah," I said, "I saw him. I'm gonna say hi." Buzz was across the room talking with Marcy and Chad. Marcy was Henry Brookman's daughter. She was on the board. Chad did the front office. They nodded over at us and we waved.

"And some perennials, too," she said. "Randy, Denise, Kwame . . ."

I could hear Denise's squeal in the hallway. She was a hoot. She could get people in stitches in about three seconds. She was one of the first people I knew at UCS. Actually, I knew her before I was at UCS.

I was standing there holding a bottle of pop David had opened for me. A line was forming behind me.

Denise's husband, Norm, had died in '85. He was an old friend of my old friend Jim. It blew me away when Jim died.

Suddenly I felt like there wasn't any time. I didn't want to not say it. "Margaret," I said, "I'm sorry you're sick."

Everyone was loud around us. David was talking to the guy next to him. They were talking about California, where the guy grew up, so I didn't know if Margaret had heard me, but her face softened.

"Thank you," she said quietly.

"You're a great person, Margaret, you're really great. If there's anything I can do—"

She looked at me a few seconds, she looked so grateful. "Thank you," she said again, like she was glad to be talking about it.

But then we heard David telling the guy next to him about his and Margaret's plan to take their kids to Disneyland the summer after next when their eldest graduated from grade school. When I heard him say "summer after next" my eyes shot over to him. It was only for a second, but Margaret caught it. She saw me wonder how long she had to live.

I wanted to apologize to her but I couldn't say anything.

She hadn't stopped looking at me. "There is something you can do," she said.

She put her hand up to my cheek and I remembered the way she'd touched my face that time she and I were with Rick. I felt her hand against my skin. She said, "You can hope again."

THE GIFT OF
MOURNING

C onnie had really gone downhill. She'd gone from where she could hobble around with her cane and try to act cheery to where she couldn't get out of bed without somebody's help. Then she just stayed like that a while, like she was on hold.

Joe brought Miss Kitty over to see her. The docs had said it was OK, that it wouldn't make any difference at that point. Connie was really happy to see her cat again, she'd missed her. Miss Kitty went straight to Connie's bed and jumped right up with her. Connie was in a hospital bed in the living room where she'd moved because when they took out the overstuffed chairs and just kept the TV, there was more room for the IV stand and all the medical gear. So when Miss Kitty jumped on the bed with Connie like everything was still normal, Connie loved it.

Joe stayed that night at the house. He told Connie the next morning he'd had to because he didn't want to wake Miss Kitty from her beauty rest to take her back to his and Tony's place. Connie let Joe get away with the line about Miss Kitty, she even laughed. Before she had always been adamant about not wanting Joe or any of the kids to move back in to take care of her. "They all have their own lives" was her line. But the docs had said Connie needed someone there twenty-four hours because she shouldn't spend the night in the house alone. No one wanted to hire someone to sleep there so when Joe and Miss Kitty stayed over Connie didn't argue. Still, no one in the family ever said the words Joe had "moved back in." They said he was just "staying over." Even after Tony had moved in too.

So Joe and Tony were living there, just going back to their apartment to get mail and new clothes, etc. They were living in Joe's old room he'd grown up in. The room had bunk beds. They took the top one down and moved them together. The room was very crowded, a boy's room with two grown men living in it. The walls still had Joe's soccer posters from high school and his Glee Club medals and boys' books on the shelves. But there were also the guys' briefcases and Tony's cellular phone and their ties and suits and wing tips in the closet. Connie and John's old room would have fit their things better, but Joe wouldn't move into his mother's, his mother and father's, room.

Tony and Joe tried to make the place like home again for Connie. They made regular dinners and ate them at the dining room table. Tony would do his casseroles and Italian things, and Joe would fix things they'd eaten when they were growing up—pot roast and mashed potatoes and beans. Once he even made pancakes with Diane's syrup. Joe would bring Connie to the table and they'd try to help her eat or drink a smoothie. Ingrid came over as often as she could. If she couldn't get a sitter she'd bring the twins and I'd hang out with them while Connie and her kids and Tony ate.

I was over there all the time. I arrived early in the morning, usually about when the guys were heading out to work. They'd have had something to eat and washed their own dishes. Joe was very tidy and completely neurotic that I would never do their dishes or laundry but only help out with Connie. His line was that he didn't want to "take advantage" of me. He was just like his mother. So I'd see the guys in the morning and they'd tell me how Connie had been in the night—she rarely slept all the way through anymore—and if there was anything special for me to look out for or tell the nurse. Then they'd go to work.

The last thing before they went to work, Joe would take his coffee over and sit by Connie's bed and visit with her. He wouldn't try to get her to eat or take her meds, but only talk about normal things, things in the newspaper, his or Tony's work, the cat, whatever. Then when it was time for work, Tony'd come in and spread out his arms and give Connie a huge hug and a loud kiss on the forehead and say, "Ciao, Mamma Connie!" or "See you tonight at bootie class." Tony was having Connie teach and work with him on some booties for Diane's baby that was due. Connie hadn't done any knitting on her own for a while, and she got a kick out of Tony, who was such a muscle man, knitting. Connie always said she loved how energetic Tony was and she told me once, not in front of them, how good she thought he was for Joe. So Tony'd say bye to Connie and Joe'd lean over and kiss her on the cheek and say, "See you this evening, Mom." He'd say it so earnestly, like he was afraid he wouldn't. Then Tony'd coax Joe out to work. Joe was going downhill in his own way too.

After the guys left for work I'd clean Connie up, change her nightie and diaper and the sheets and give her a sponge bath and try to get her to eat or drink something. She liked it when she could get things down. She said they felt good on her throat.

Often when I washed her she would close her eyes, sometimes she even slept. But other times she watched. Not just my hands where I was washing her, but me. I felt nervous, like I should stop, but when I asked her, "Connie, is something wrong?" she said, "No, everything's fine, I just want to see." She was watching things very carefully, lovingly, because she wanted to remember them because she knew she would be leaving.

Connie had accepted things. She seemed like she

was almost ready. It was Joe who was having a harder time.

Once when I was on my way back into the kitchen with a food tray and Joe and Tony were in there, I heard Tony say something about "Connie's room," and Joe snapped, "It's not *Connie's* room, it's the sick room, dammit." I stopped outside the door. I was holding a tray she hadn't eaten from. I heard someone put something down on a cabinet and then Tony say very quietly, "Joe. Honey. Joey." Then Joe started to say something but his voice cracked. Then he was crying, then the crying was muffled. That was Tony holding Joe and Joe crying into Tony's chest. I'd seen them hold each other like that before. I looked down at the tray. The protein smoothie was separating, little globs of white from the watery yellow. A pool of water had sweated off the glass of cranberry juice. The oatmeal had a skin and spoon tracks and the spoon had sunk down into it. Then I heard Joe blow his nose and say, "I'm OK, I'm OK," and turn the water on in the sink and I went in.

Connie had gotten very thin. She spent most of her time in bed. She didn't watch TV much anymore, she just lay there and looked and remembered. I tried to get her to stand up each day and sit in a chair or walk down the hall to the bathroom—the nurse who came every day said I still should—but it was hard for

Connie. She got bedsores. Her muscles felt like putty or like something in a sack. Her skin hung off her like crepe paper. It was yellow-gray, but purple and white in some places. When I touched it, it was completely smooth, and it completely gave to me. Sometimes I couldn't believe the skin was alive, I couldn't believe it was part of her.

One morning when I pulled down the sheet to wash her, her legs looked so strange. They looked utterly foreign, like something I'd never seen before. They looked horrible. Then suddenly Connie groaned. It was a sound of something living, and I looked at her face and remembered her, and I recognized her legs. Then I remembered what I was here to do, and I poured the water over her and washed her.

Ingrid brought the twins to see her from time to time. She didn't want to keep them in the dark, but she didn't want to rub their faces in it, they were only nine. Usually the kids were OK, but sometimes when they were frightened they acted like it. They'd hide behind Ingrid when she was trying to get them to talk to their grandmom. Once Tina was going up to kiss Connie good night but before she got to the bed she ran back to Ingrid and threw her arms around her legs and cried. Then Jack wouldn't budge. The kids hadn't learned to act the way everyone else was trying to.

Ingrid was very gracious about it. She held and comforted her kids while they clung to her body. She talked them out of their fear and Connie out of her sadness and shame about frightening them. I was glad Ingrid was there between them. But then when she turned to go home, and I saw the backs of the three of them, the mom flanked closely by her two kids, I saw Margaret's kids, and thought of them not being her grandchildren but her own children. I thought of how it would be for them for their mother to get sick and die when they were young. Then how it would be for Margaret's husband without her.

There was always a hole when someone died. It was always in the middle of people.

Diane and Bob were going to fly out as soon after Diane had the baby as she could. The baby was due any minute. Everyone was hoping the timing would work out. Connie spent a lot of time on the phone with Diane.

One morning when I was scooping out gel to put on Connie's bedsore, she said, "I'm lucky."

I thought I hadn't heard her right. "Lucky?"

"Yes." Her voice was very thin.

I got the gel out slowly so I could hear her.

"I'm old," she said. "I've lived a whole life. I'm dying in my time."

I stood there with the gel on my gloves, not moving. Connie rolled over a little and lifted her nightie the way I usually did to put the gel on. I pulled the nightie up the rest of the way.

"I'm not like these poor young people who die before their parents do. That's tragic. For a child to die before their parents isn't natural."

I spread the gel. I felt the warmth of her skin through the cool of it.

"And I'm lucky because I've known," she said. "I've known for a long time, so I've been able to talk to everyone or see them and tell them I love them."

I felt her skin shift through my gloves. The skin of the sore was purple and white and a couple of inches around. It was warmer than the regular skin.

"It's not like a car crash or a heart attack or something sudden when no one's ready." She took a deep breath. I stopped doing the gel. "John died of a heart attack. . . . There were things left unresolved. He hadn't seen Joe in ages. And he'd only met Tony that once."

I hadn't known any of this before, but I understood.

She turned her head to look out the window. The curtains were closed. I covered the gel and the sore with the wrap and fixed the nightie and helped her up onto her pillows.

"Should I open the curtains?" I asked.

"Thanks," she said.

I tossed my gloves in the bucket and opened the curtains. The light felt good. I got her some water and a straw. She took a drink and said, "It's terrible to die if you're angry with someone, or if you have a misunderstanding. The person left alive feels guilty, and it's hard for them to grieve for the dead person. Grief is necessary. You have to be able to mourn."

"Yes," I said, "you do."

She licked her lips and I gave her some more water and wiped her chin.

"I learned a lot from John's death," she went on. "I wish he and Joe had been able to see through their differences before John died. I know they'd have come to understand and forgive each other." Her voice shook. "It's been very hard on Joe." Her mouth was trembling.

I put my hand on her arm and said, "Joe'll be OK, Connie."

"I hope so," she said.

I stayed with her by her bed until she slept. When I went to clean up, my hands felt strange. I felt like there was something tingling inside my skin or hanging from the tips of my fingers. It felt like fibers of underwater plants, like everything was underwater, I was, and Connie was, breathing and all, but even when we weren't touching I could still feel something pulling and pressing around my body like a current of water around us.

*   *   *

I remember the frilly curtains on the windows of Connie's house. They were closed and I remember the foggy sun against the glass and I remember thinking, "I've got to wash those windows."

I let myself in with my set of Connie's keys. As soon as I was inside the house, before I took my keys out of the lock, Tony was in the hallway: "Call Ingrid." Then he was back in the living room. I went to the phone. Suddenly my skin was wet and I could feel my heartbeat. I remember the pads of my fingertips against the cool smooth buttons of the phone. Everything moved very slowly and clearly. The phone rang only twice. When she picked it up I said, "Ingrid—," and she said immediately, "I'll be right over." She lived across town, it would take her about twenty, maybe thirty minutes with the traffic. I put the phone down in the cradle and went to the living room.

Joe and Tony were standing by the same side of the bed. Joe was holding Connie's hands. Tony was standing behind Joe with one hand on Joe's back and the other on Connie's and Joe's hands. Connie's mouth was open. Her eyes were wide and startled-looking. When he heard me at the door, Tony nodded over to the other side of the bed. I came into the room and stood on that side of the bed. Connie was blinking very quickly and her eyes always opened wide. Her mouth, her jaw, was trembling. Her lower lip was tight and white. Joe was looking at Connie. He kept looking at her as he lifted her right hand in his left and handed it over to me. I took her hand. Then Joe took Tony's right in his left, then Tony reached his free hand across the bed and took mine and we were a circle.

I could feel the cool round pads of the insides of Connie's fingers and the smoothness of her palm. Tony gripped my hand tightly and I felt his ring that matches Joe's. Tony looked at Connie then at Joe. Connie's mouth was still open but her eyes weren't blinking as quickly. Her breathing was in rasps. Joe's mouth was open too, and trembling, but he wasn't making any noise. Tony looked back at Connie, then at Joe. Then Tony took a slow, deep breath: in then out, in then out. Then Tony said, his voice was very calm, "We're here, Connie. You can let go whenever you want."

Connie's throat made a watery noise. Tony took another deep breath, in then out, then he closed his eyes. I could smell the sweat of all of us, and something else, very faint and sweet. Tony squeezed my hand again and I squeezed back, then I squeezed Connie's too. Tony kept breathing slow and deep. Then, Joe started to breathe like that too, slow and deep. After Joe breathed like that for a while, Connie's breath changed too, it slowed and became deeper, and it became clear, not gurgling.

Joe and his mother looked at one another. Then Joe

got his voice. It was very calm, like Tony's. Joe said, "We're here, Mom, we're all here with you, Ingrid and Diane too, and we all love you, Mom, and Dad too." He breathed in then out and said slowly, determined she should understand, "Dad's here too, Mom, and he'll be there with you and it's all OK. It's all OK, Mom. You can go whenever you want. It's all OK."

Joe sounded old and understanding as he talked to her. He was helping her leave the world she'd brought him into.

Connie closed her eyes slowly but then opened them fast again. She didn't want to stop seeing yet.

"It's OK, Mom," Joe said. "We're all together. Whenever you want, Mom."

Connie looked very closely at Joe, and he looked back at her the same. Then she closed her eyes and no one spoke and there was only the sound of us breathing. Joe watched his mother rest. He closed his eyes.

Then there was a pause and a breath, then a watery sound, and Connie's jaw snapped open and there was a gasp, a rattle, and her jaw went slack and still and she was still.

After a while, Joe said, again, "It's OK, Mom. You can go whenever you want."

Joe's eyes were still closed.

Tony looked over at Joe. When Joe stopped to take a breath, Tony said, "Joe, she's gone."

But Joe said, louder, like Tony'd interrupted him,

"It's OK, Mom, we're here. It's OK, Mom—" Then his voice cracked. Tears were welling up in his eyes.

Tony said, "Open your eyes, Joe, you have to look." Then, when Joe didn't, Tony said, "Joe, she's gone."

Joe's face was red and wet but he wasn't making any sound. He was keeping his eyes shut tight. Tony loosened his hand from mine and stepped behind Joe. He put his arms around Joe and held him and rocked him. Joe was still holding his mother's hand. I was still holding her other hand. Tony helped Joe sit down on the bed by his mother. I reached over and put Connie's hand I was holding into Joe's. Joe held both her hands in his. He held them loosely, as if he wanted them to move, but they were still.

Joe lifted his head and wailed. The wail was a huge long sound like an animal. Tony bent over to hold Joe more. When Joe was sobbing more normally Tony stood up and Joe leaned forward and bowed his head. His shoulders shook. Tony put his hand on Joe's back.

After a few seconds Tony looked over at me and we stepped away from the bed.

Ingrid arrived. She stood in the living room door like she was frozen. Tony went over and held her then brought her into the room. Ingrid knelt down by the bed. Joe took one of his sister's hands. They lay against their mother's breast and wept.

Tony and I went out of the room. We left them with the body and they mourned.

A C K N O W L E D G M E N T S

"The Gift of Sweat" first appeared in *Good to Go* (Zero Hour Publications, 1994).

Thanks to the Chicken Soup Brigade and the Home Care Program at Fremont Public Association, two agencies that provide practical help for people living with AIDS and other disabilities. Ten percent of the author's royalties from this book are being tithed to Fremont. Thanks especially to Katherine Ravenscroft.

Thanks to the MacDowell Colony. A residency there in autumn 1992 gave me the time and place to begin writing this book.

Thanks to Amy Scholder, Harold Schmidt, and Joy Johannessen, for faith in my work.

Love and thanks again to Mom, George, and Aldo.

To Chris Galloway: Thanks for the gift of the heart.

This is for Claude.